The Sm

MW01132438

by Mitch Bouchette

This is a work of fiction dedicated to Lisette, my bride of 35+ years; who inspires me, motivates me, and challenges me; she gives my life real meaning.

ACKNOWLEDGMENTS: Cover art provided by "Painting Delores LLC." The artist, Delores Lusk, is a remarkably talented lady whose work is on display at the "Elephant Ear Art Gallery" in Sumter, SC. If you are interested please check out their website at "http://www.theelephanteargallery.com/" - or - drop the artist a e-mail at "dclusk01@gmail.com".

And, I would be remiss not to thank Ken and Adele, owners of the "real" Pink Sand Cottage in North Palmetto Point, Eleuthra, BH. It is with their consent I share this little bit of paradise they created. The place and the feelings it inspires last forever. This book is fiction, but the cottage is real with soft breezes and gentle rains . . . and there is real tangible magic there.

About The Author: Mitch Bouchette brings a wealth of background knowledge and experience from his travels throughout Europe, Africa, Latin America and South West Asia. He is a linguist and has an insatiable curiosity; so it is not surprising he has made a lifetime study of people and places and weaves his observations into his writing.

Action Titles From The Author:

The Sword Of Rule: Newen's Sword

Gaelin's Raid: The Sword Of Rule Viking Series Book 2

Southern Rules (Book 1)

More Southern Rules (Book 2)

Tango Section Operative # 5 (Book 1): Rescue From Iran

Tango Section: Survival! (Book 2)

Romance Titles From The Author

The Smell Of Rain: Romance As It Should Be

Feel The Rain: Romance Rekindled As It Should Be

After The Rain: Romance In The Time Of COVID

1. ERICA: THINKING ABOUT IT

There are some things you need to know right from the start. First among the things you need to know is that the island is beautiful; not beautiful like a nice post card your favorite aunt sends you from Miami, oh no! This island is drop dead gorgeous, take your breath away, beautiful. Oh, I will freely admit that it may be a little off the beaten path, but that is a good thing, a very good thing. This is a good thing because it means the island is not invaded every year by Euro-trash or fake wanna'-be famous "TV personalities."

What the island is, is beautiful in a natural unspoiled sort of way, not tacky or glitzy, and not fake. It is just beautiful and it is real. Yeah, that's the word I was looking for, "real." The sunrises and sunsets are real and the beach is real, and unfortunately some times of the year the mosquitoes are real. But the wind comes in off the water, really it's just a gentle breeze, and the mosquitoes disappear. Oh, that reminds me, I didn't tell you about the journals, or diaries or whatever they are, where people have recorded their opinions and experiences on the island and in the cottage.

One of my favorite comments came from an entry from some unknown previous guest at the cottage. It went something like this, "Just get over it and use the damn mosquito repellent! Then enjoy the view." Now, for me personally, I never had a problem with the mosquitoes but I did find the series of mismatched diary-journals useful to guide my explorations of the island.

And, by "explorations" I mean searching out places

3

to eat with a good view and with good food. Sorry, I got sidetracked there for a minute, where was I? Oh yeah, I was telling you some things about the island, by the way, thanks for your patience.

****

The sun is brighter than anywhere else you have ever been; and the wind, like I said, is more of a gentle caress than a gust; and the sky has more stars at night than anywhere else in the world. The palm trees are prettier than any place else and the sand is a lovely shade of pink. That's right, pink! The pink sand comes from thousands of years of the beach waves, driven by the tides, grinding old shells and coral into dust and resettling it on the Atlantic side along the coast. There are flamingos and iguanas and "blue holes" into which you can dive. And of course there are the caverns to explore above ground and hundreds of kinds of flora and fauna. It is the Bahamas – or at least a part of the Bahamas, but it is called Eleuthra, not Nassau, and in this case that was also a good thing.

It was a good thing because she, Erica, had been to the Bahamas before and even at her young age; she had already had enough of the fast life and glitz. Even so, when John invited her, she hesitated and in fact only gave in to him finally because of the pictures and the tone of his voice as he described each scene.

John had started showing her the pictures over a cup of coffee in the sitting area on the second floor of the old College Bookstore on DOG Street in Williamsburg. DOG was the acronym all the "from-heres" used to identify themselves as locals and one more way to separate themselves from the non-locals who they called "come-heres." The come-heres were like tourists who didn't know when to go back home to where they came from. So "DOG Street" was a kind of snobby shorthand for the Duke of Gloucester Street in Colonial Williamsburg, Virginia.

John stole glances at Erica's eyes and face, looking for telltale signs of reaction as he explained to her that he had shot the photos a few years ago on his last trip to the islands with a diving group. She liked him. He was sweet and sincere and sometimes he explained things that he didn't need to explain; but he did it in a sweet sort of way that was almost shy.

She liked him so much that she wanted to be alone with him. But of course she did not tell him that. she told him she would consider coming with him to the islands because the pictures showed an island experience that promised to be just too good to pass up.

****

Perhaps she was considering it because he gave her such a different vibe from the other guys in her life. Perhaps she just felt that this might be different from her previous trips to the Bahamas a couple of years ago. Don't get me wrong; Nassau is a wonderful place for most of the tourists who visit Bahamas. Obviously a significant percentage of the world's island vacation population agrees with that assessment because about three quarters of them live in or around Nassau it seems. But Erica had already seen Nassau, even if it was mostly from a beach towel through dark glasses nursing a hangover and waiting for the sun to go down.

On that previous trip, a couple of years ago, she had drunk entirely too many big drinks with little umbrellas in them. She had also shown entirely too much skin to too many people and had come back home with a sunburn and some blurry, indistinct memories. She also brought home a broken heart that took a long, long time to heal. But this, "new thing" with this "new guy," had a different feel about it. And she was considering it, and she was considering John.

She was "trying the idea on" to see if it fit her, so to speak. She had looked up Eleuthra from idle curiosity on the web and she found that the island only had about eight thousand people and that the name derived form a Greek word meaning "free." Somehow that appealed to her too. She needed to get away from Williamsburg, Virginia and its people right now and the idea of being "free" was exactly what she thought she needed. She was right but she did not yet know just how right she was.

****

Eleuthra is 110 miles long and about one mile wide and there are plenty of empty spaces to just sit and watch the sea and sort out your thoughts. She thought that might be a good thing because she had not yet decided what all of her thoughts and feelings were about John.

Oh, he was good-looking and fit. In fact he spent enough time in the gym or pursuing outdoor and indoor sports that he was very fit -- with powerful shoulders, a wide chest and a flat stomach. Actually, that was part of the problem. A couple of years ago, if she had met John, she would have thought of him as eye-candy, and maybe regarded him as fun for a casual liaison. But this year she was looking for a deeper commitment and she wasn't sure they were in the same place emotionally. And, she just wasn't sure about his level of commitment, at least not yet, no matter how good the early indications were.

Of course, Erica reasoned, this might be a good way to feel him out about many things. After all a week in a one-room cottage, alone with him might be a good way to find out a lot of things. Even if it was a large, well appointed one-room efficiency apartment really, and on the beach, and I mean right on the beach, there was just no place to hide from each other. There were things she wanted to know about him and things she wanted to know about herself.

****

In truth, Erica still harbored hard feelings almost two years later over her last affair and did not yet understand why her previous lover, Brad, had just dumped her. He had used the standard line, "Oh, it's not you. It's me." But what the heck was that supposed to mean anyway? And given Brad's narcissistic tendencies it was definitely not about him -- he loved himself a little too much for that. So she knew that, regardless of what he had said, the break up was most certainly about her – about her not being good enough for him.

It really did bother her that she did not know why their relationship had failed. He came from a good family, and for that matter so did she. He had family money, but so did she. Hell, she thought, everyone in Williamsburg had money, or so it seemed.

****

But, back to the present she told herself she had to live in the "now" and focus on the present. The cottage, John had told her, " . . . was such a quaint little place nestled in a tropical paradise." And the pictures certainly bore witness to the raw beauty of the place.

She would find out when they got there just how much thought had gone into the place, its location and its construction.

The owners, he had told her, had set it up from construction to decoration to be a little bit of heaven, and a haven from the outside world. She did not yet know that she would in fact marvel at the authenticity and rawness of the island. She would also marvel at the natural way the people seemed to exist in a happy cooperative relationship with the land and the sea and with each other.

The place was all unspoiled beaches that inspired the visitor to just slow down, take a deep breath, relax and smell the air. She would be able to smell the salt air from the Atlantic and the musky aura of the pre-dawn breeze across the land that filtered through the trees and lush vegetation. And, she would be able to smell the rain when it was blowing in off the water on its way to them. Before the stay was over that would be her favorite smell because it invariably served to drive them back to the covered porch of the cottage and eventually into the bedchamber; but that would be later. First she had to come to grips with her own thoughts, and fears and doubts.

Erica had "scar tissues" from being "burned" in that previous relationship, but that was no fault of the Bahamas. That was the fault of . . . what? What had she missed? When had it turned into a purely physical relationship with Brad?

She felt used, and she had been angry and had said to herself that she would never go to the islands again. But that had been unrealistic; she knew the problem had been Brad and her, not the islands. In fact it had nothing to do with the islands.

The left over feelings she had from that last trip to the Bahamas were an indication of how much she liked John, that she would even consider going back there with him. Of course this was not Nassau and this was not nightlife and glitz. We'll see, she thought. We'll see.

****

2. ART & SAM: ARRIVAL
... back Again ...

Arthur and Samantha sat across from each other in the slightly crowded and slightly cramped cabin of the Silver Air flight from Fort Lauderdale, Florida to Governor's Harbor, Eleuthra, Bahamas. The flight was pleasant, even if a little tight, because it was a short flight and everyone on board was happy. You know, it is amazing what you can tolerate when there are smiles involved. And, why wouldn't they be happy, after all they were all going to the islands.

Everyone on board was going to be in the sun on a beach today, and they knew it, and that fact can be a serious motivator for good attitudes. Arthur sat across from Samantha in the aisle seat because he was trying to get a little extra legroom for his seventy year old, six foot four inch frame. Samantha sat upright looking like a queen.

Samantha had always taken care of herself and was looking to be a very trim and very fit lady of sixty or so. He glanced over at her and felt his heart flutter like the first time he had ever seen her. She looked good with grey hair cut short and well styled and wearing a white linen top shirt and pants, set off with a pair of expensive looking sandals. She looked comfortable in the airplane seats that, for her at least, were a good fit.

Sam, as he called her, leaned over and touched his arm. He leaned closer to hear, "Art," she said just loud enough for him to hear her words, "we look like we are here as the chaperones for this group."

"Sam," he answered with a grin that could still make her smile, "that's only because they haven't seen you in your bikini!" and he winked at her. "They don't know what a wild woman you really are." That was an inside joke between the two of them. Samantha had worked hard her whole life and followed all the rules and done everything "right," including building a successful business before Art had ever met her.

Somehow he had touched her in a way and in a place deep in her soul that no one else ever had. It was not that he had just come along at the right time. It had been the right time but it was so much more than that. She had never felt so cared for and so free to do what she felt like doing. Throwing caution to the wind was just not a part of her persona; or so she thought. In fact their first weekend away together, she had a little to much to drink and, based on a cell phone video Art offered as evidence the next morning, she had somehow wound up dancing on a table the night before.

In the morning, he was waiting on the edge of the bed with a cup of coffee and a couple of aspirins and filled in the details on which she was unclear from the night before. Sam had been mortified but as the day wore on, and her hangover subsided, she also realized that Art had been there and had gotten her back to the room safely and had been there in the morning to support her and he did not judge her. But he also had not let her forget her first and last night as a "wild woman!"

Sam hit him on the arm and she felt his biceps tense in anticipation of her punch. "You know exactly what I mean. Most of these people could be our kids and some are clearly the age of your grandkids . . ."

He cut her off, "Sorry, I wasn't listening. I just keep thinking about your tight little butt in that bikini."

Now it was her turn to tease him, "Who said I was going to be wearing anything at all? The cottage is not near anyone and we know we could very well spend all day on the porch and never see another living soul."

"See," Art said, "that's the wild woman I was talking about!"

****

"Ladies and gentlemen," the flight attendant cut them both off through the tiny metallic sounding speaker above their heads, " please prepare for landing at Governor's Harbor. We will be on the ground shortly." And, they were.

Samantha barely had time to reflect on what he had said - wild woman, indeed! Samantha had never been a wild woman. There was no hidden collection of old photos in a shoebox someplace showing her in a wet T-shirt contest during spring break in college. In fact she had only ever seen one wet T-shirt contest and she definitely had not participated! She had always been the good girl who did all the assignments in school and who was always properly attired for Mass on Sunday morning. She had never had a "Goth-period" or a "Biker-period" or for that matter she also did not have a "tramp stamp tattoo" on her rear.

Oh, she had had her share of old lovers but the relationships, while intense in their own right, were really pretty conservative affairs, at least before she met Art. Being with him somehow made her feel "safe enough" to let go a little; maybe it was all that time he had spent in the military and in command of something or other. He exuded confidence and capability and she knew he had experienced some really intense combat situations but he never talked about them; and she liked that about him too. Frankly she found that quiet self-assured confidence attractive.

It was not that he had somehow given her permission to let go; it was that ever since he had walked into her coffee shop, he was just always there for her and he had always been there for her. If anything, with him around she had given herself permission to let go, and it was a very empowering feeling. Deep down inside she knew this trip was as much for her as it was for him. She squeezed his bicep one more time during the touchdown as the little plane landed, because she wanted to and it felt reassuring.

****

It was a smooth landing with one little bump as they touched down. Art was happy to be out of the little twin-engine turboprop aircraft and standing erect. He stretched and towered over Samantha for just a second then picked up their bags and the two slightly wrinkled but tanned and distinguished looking senior citizens headed across the tarmac in a one minute walk to the metal building.

****

Sam and Art knew this process very well and entered the metal building that looked like a mid-sized warehouse. It was a very basic structure but it housed customs and immigration in one large room and then ticket sales and departures in the other large room on the other side of a metal wall separating them. This was the entire international side of the airport. The national side of the airport was across the parking lot about a hundred yards away and was housed in similar metal buildings, but it was all in one big open space.

Art stepped forward, but not too far forward, with

Sam at his side as he held out the passports to the immigration officer at the makeshift desk at the end of the long red line painted on the floor. The tall black woman behind the desk smiled a familiar smile and said, "Welcome back, Mr. Arthur and Mrs. Samantha, we have missed your smiling faces, how long will you be here this time?" She seemed content with the answer and waived them across the red line painted on the concrete floor of the building so that they could "enter" the country and move to the customs desk.

Before they could take the five steps to the next makeshift desk, Jamison had appeared through the doorway, taken their bags and placed them on the low table and then stepped to one side to allow the customs official to do her job. The next official they encountered was another tall black woman. The first time Samantha had come here she had thought how this woman could easily have been the sister, if not the twin of the first lady. She had learned later that the two officials were in fact sisters. Samantha noted that even as she and Art moved to the second lady's station, the first lady still watched Jamison a little too closely and a little too often for it to be casual interest. Sam knew the two were married and it always brought a smile to her lips to think how much their love must be like the one she and Art shared.

Jamison was a tall thin black man who was a natural born Eleutheran. Art and Sam had been renting cars from him on every trip for the past ten years. The first time they came here the precise relationship between Jamison and the two ladies was not exactly a mystery because it was obvious they had some sort of relationship. After all, Jamison Smith's customers seemed to get their baggage first and clear through immigration and customs first, or at least with minimum hassle.

But, it had taken about three trips here, over a couple of years for Jamison to open up and reveal to them that he was married to the lady at the immigration station whose name was Sunny. And, he had explained that the lady at the customs station was his sister-in-law, whose name was Sweetness. But it took another year still to learn that Sweetness lived with Sunny and Jamison. "It's a big house and Sweetness has her own little apartment in the place." Jamison had explained.

In fact this was pretty typical of Eleutherans who seemed to always find amicable and practical solutions to life's little problems. People just took care of people here and while they got the things done, it was at their own pace and no one seemed to mind.

****

And pretty soon Jamison was helping Art and Sam load their bags into the back of an old Jeep Cherokee, which had the one obligatory bald tire, and with the air conditioner that mostly worked. They drove carefully on the wrong side of the street from the airport to the one major intersection that served as the business center of the town. And, they managed to avoid being hit by two large trucks and one motorized bicycle as they cut in to park at the Waters Store on the route to the Cottage.

Inside the Waters Store, the wife, Mrs. Waters, seemed to be presiding over the stocking and sale of everything one would need for a short or a long stay on the island. The husband, Mr. Waters, occupied the other half of the building and "held court" presiding over the sale of beer and wine and even some hard liquor. The Waters Store was an absolute must before getting to the cottage so they took their time; greeted everyone and stocked up on the critical elements – beer, wine and basic food.

Art was smiling and enjoying the whole adventure and had even pushed the "other thing" to the back of his mind. Sam was smiling too, but she was watching Art from the corner of her eye. She was still very much in love with this man after thirty years. He was handsome, strong, successful in everything he did, and in fact everything he had ever done.

****

As she maneuvered through the store between and among the packed shelves with very little space between them, Art told her, using hand signals, that he was going next door to get some wine and beer. She just smiled and waved at him and he went out the front door and turned immediately back into the building through the other door into the beer shop.

When she had collected what they needed and paid for the bags, she put the food in the back of the jeep with the help of the owner's son. Then she walked from the back of the Jeep and entered the beer shop and found Art leaning against the counter drinking a Kalik beer with the owner. Sam stopped in the doorway with her hands on her hips looking sternly into a room full of men. She had not said a word when the men scattered away from the two men drinking. Both of whom looked appropriately guilty.

"Baby, Sam, don't be angry, it was Johnson's fault. He made me." Art said to her as she suppressed a smile.

"Mrs. Samantha, that is a bold face lie this

scoundrel has told you! It was he who demanded, demanded I tell you, that I give him a sample of the beer he had just bought but not yet paid for! And, I as a humble merchant, afraid of losing the sale that would so benefit my family; well, I was intimidated and yielded to his demands." Johnson Waters said with a smile in his voice.

Then turning to Art he said in a stage whisper, "Let's see you get out of that one!"

"Oh, I have no doubt where the fault lies, Mr. Waters, I have been suffering with this man for over thirty years. I suppose I should not be surprised that he left me to fend for myself with all those groceries while he was here treating your fine establishment like a common bar." Then as she looked sternly around the room the other men, all of whom had an open beer bottle, quietly and quickly moved the bottles behind their backs starting to smile back at her as the little drama played out. When she finished the slow look around the room, she spoke again, "Why, the only two bottles I see are the ones in front of you two!" with a little mock scorn in her voice.

"Well, fellows, since I am already in trouble I guess I should finish this beer and get out of here." Art raised the bottle and finished the last swallow and placed the bottle on the counter. "Thanks, Johnson, we will get together again before she makes me leave this paradise. But just for the record, I have never seen you intimidated by anyone any time." The other man all raised their bottles and took a long draught as Art and Sam walked out arm in arm.

Johnson spoke to everyone in general and no one in particular, "I have missed them. Glad they are back."

Art and Sam drove from the store down the road, up the hill, and on to the end of the pavement, holding hands. They touched each other on the leg, or on the hand or on the shoulder as they chatted about nothing in particular. Both were very happy to be back in a place where they had shared so much love and so many good memories. The two of them were like so many other foreign visitors and tourists to the island who had found a happy place in a world of chaos on this island in this archipelago.

****

Of course these days no-one is truly indigenous to Eleuthra. The original populations were people of the Taino and were members of the Arawak Nation. But they were deported en masse by the Spaniards to work in the fields and mines of the island of Hispaniola, which now is modern day Haiti and Dominican Republic. The working conditions in those days were harsh and the Taino either perished from the hard labor or from the infectious diseases. The Europeans brought the diseases with them and the Taino had no resistance against them.

These original inhabitants were wiped out in a mere sixty years from about 1490 to 1550. By the time the next wave of European settlers arrived in 1648 the island is thought to have been uninhabited. Very little remains, and even an intact ritual seat, called a duo, which was discovered in the 19th century has been moved to the British Museum.

These Puritan Pilgrims arrived from Bermuda as the "Eleutherian Adventurers" from whom the island takes its name. As we said, Eleutheria is a Greek word meaning freedom and the "Adventurers" came for the purpose of building a free land for themselves. The settlements remain today from north to south along the island with names like The Bluff, Upper and Lower Bogue, Current, Gregory Town, Alice Town, James Cistern, Governor's Harbour, North and South Palmetto Point, Savannah Sound, and Winding Bay. And, there is Tarpum Bay, Rock Sound, Greencastle, Deep Creek, Delancy Town, Waterford, Wemyss Bight, John Millars, Millar's and Bannerman Town. The airports are at North Eleuthra, Governor's Harbour, and Rock Sound with flights to the United States and the rest of the archipelago.

When the Bahamas became independent from Britain in 1973, they did a lot of things right and a lot of things wrong. In hindsight one of the wrong things may have been imposition of new laws forcing large resorts and agricultural businesses to sell out to government-favored Bahamian interests. These repressive laws had the effect one might imagine – those who could leave, left. The capitol flight that followed quickly meant the most prosperous and prominent residents just left and took their money, talent and skills with them. This started an economic downturn as businesses were, in some cases, just abandoned.

Then as tax laws in the United States changed again in the early 1980s an already bad situation just got worse. The changes to they laws just exacerbated the situation, and more businesses failed. However what did not "fail" was the natural raw beauty of Hatchet Bay caves, or Surfer's Beach, or Ocean Hole. Today the primary settlements are Governor's Harbour (which is also the administrative capital of the Island),

Rock Sound, Tarpum Bay, Harbour Island and Spanish Wells.

What had first attracted a younger version of Arthur and Samantha and inspired them to come here were the unique pink sand beaches of the island. Tens of thousands of years of waves rubbing and pounding conch shells against coral reefs, and then depositing the powdery remains on the shore gave the beaches a beautiful and distinctive pink tint. Samantha had found the perfect place to experience this awesome scene when she found the Pink Sand Cottage available for rental.

****

The cottage dominated her thoughts again today as Art moved the jeep more slowly now off the paved road and through the narrow lane. The lane was really just two ruts making their way through an encroaching jungle of flowers and vines and palm trees. This went on for several miles with occasional wide spots in the road to allow opposing motorists to negotiate passage.

This was definitely not Nassau! But for the two of them it was a "way better place." In fact it is a way better place for those who, like them, wanted to get off the beaten path with someone special and just be alone to enjoy each other's company.

The cottages and houses were spaced along the beach at about quarter mile intervals and that meant it was very likely the only footprints you would see on the sand were your own. OK, that might be an exaggeration, but seeing more than one or two other couples in a day of strolling on the beach was a rarity, and the sand really is pink!

After about 10 minutes of the sandy road-path they

arrived at the Pink Sand Cottage nestled among the palm trees with a wide spot for parking just big enough to accommodate the Jeep. As Art set the handbrake and killed the engine, Sam had a distinct feeling of being "home."

****

"Baby," she said to Art, stopping him momentarily as he was about to exit the vehicle.

He relaxed back into the car seat and turned to her in response, "Yes?"

"Baby, thanks for bringing me here. I can't think of anyplace I would rather be or for that matter anyone I would rather be with." And, with that she leaned over, twisting in her seat, and kissed him.

"Hold that thought," he said through a warm inviting smile, "and let me get these bags into the house."

She watched closely. He had no problem lugging the suitcases through the sand. But as he started up the steep wooden steps to the cottage's back door she noticed he only carried one bag at a time. In times past he would have done the "macho-man thing" and carried two or more at a time. She immediately grabbed the smaller things and a bag of groceries and followed him up the stairs and into the kitchen blocking his attempt to return for another suitcase. "Put your arms around me and kiss me first," she commanded and he obeyed without question.

As they broke the embrace she patted his chest and said, "Why don't you get the place open or closed or air conditioned or something and figure out which key opens which doors while I get the rest of the small stuff from the car? That other big suitcase is not going

21

anyplace and the cottage will start getting comfortable faster when we get the cooling going."

"I guess you are right," he said and started fiddling with the air conditioner and the windows and the shutters. It was a good subterfuge and it kept him on one level for a few more minutes after the exertion of getting the heavy suitcase up the stairs.

More importantly, it was a valid task because some of the windows were open and some were closed and some of the wooden storm shutters outside the windows had been opened and some were closed. Regardless of whether you wanted chilled air or the ocean breeze something had to be done to make them all one way or the other way. He knew she was trying to keep him from exertion but it was somehow OK because this did have to be done.

The one thing he did not have to do anything with was to adjust the shutters. The shutters were all large boards joined by a sturdy crosspiece and painted white. The shutters over the windows were attached at the top by a board that had been hinged firmly to the side of the house. Then they had been propped open by a foot and a half long wooden props that lifted them at the bottom away from the exterior walls.

This arrangement was common in the islands. It did provide some shade and did let some air flow through the one great room of the cottage if the glass windows themselves were opened. In fact the whole thing was really quite ingenious and quite effective. In a rush to secure the place from an approaching storm it was as simple as knocking the supports down and the shutters could slam shut from their own weight.

The white paint on them stood out very pleasantly

against the light pink exterior walls of the cottage. The only difference was with the shutters on the front porch on the beachside of the cottage. These front shutters were the same heavy whitewashed wood but were mounted in the traditional way on both sides of the windows.

The pink wall and the white wood set off nicely against a relatively large natural wood floored porch on the front of the cottage. There was a white railing separating the occupants from the sea lettuce that covered the berm. That berm, covered in the lush green plant, was for erosion control to protect the beach which lay about eight feet below. And the whole effect was really quite pleasing to the eye.

If you stood at the bottom of the steep wooden steps that extended from a sunning platform off to one side of the cottage, and looked back, up at the berm, covered in green, you saw the pink walls and the white shutters and palm trees and pink sand under your feet and a beautiful clear blue water. Art stood on the porch just looking out at the ocean and down at the beach and enjoying the moment.

****

He did not hear her come up behind him but he felt her arms slide along his sides and around his midsection to hug him from behind. He felt the pressure of her breasts in his back and the warmth of her as she turned her head to one side to press her pretty face against his shoulder blades. Art reached behind himself to return the hug without disturbing her position and then his eyes popped wide open as he felt the smooth soft skin of her back and realized she was at least partially naked.

Now, he turned quickly in her arms and saw to his surprise, and pleasure, she was standing on the little porch naked in his arms framed by the open door in the middle of the wall that separated the exterior of the porch from the interior of the cottage. Over her shoulder he saw the bed that dominated the room off to his left and the sofa and chair that fit neatly on the side off to his right.

Then he looked back to the bed where he finally noticed that she had turned down the covers and he slid his big rough hands down her sides and over the mounds of her perfect butt and squeezed her cheeks ever so slightly. They stayed that way for a long, long minute. Then she broke the embrace and he followed her into the room and left the door open to feel the breeze and see the view. Nothing mattered except each other and that was the way it had been for thirty years. And, that is the way it was today; nothing mattered except her and for her nothing mattered except him.

"I guess we can let that last suitcase wait," he said through a muffled kiss.

"It can definitely wait," she said through the same kiss and pulled his shirt over his head and dropped it onto the floor.

****

3. HARRY & JANE: FRICTION IN ATLANTA

Meanwhile, half way around the world in Atlanta, Harry was ignoring the lunch plate that Jane had put in front of him as he talked in a loud voice at his phone. At least that was the way she thought of it because he never actually seemed to be talking on his phone or through his phone to real people. He just talked "at" his phone in a voice that was too often rude and too often with an edge to it. She sometimes wondered what the people on the other end of the call must have thought of him.

Jane knew what she thought of him. The glory days from college of a football hero had faded into a slightly paunchy, and sometimes overly aggressive, middle age hard-nosed businessman. Of course in fairness, to be totally honest, on balance she had to admit he was, what her mother would have called "a good provider," except regrettably for the one thing she wished he still provided – romance.

He had been so attentive and sweet in college but not these days. Now he seemed entirely focused on the expansion of his factory. Here they were just over a week away from her dream vacation for two weeks in the Bahamas at a little cottage she had found on a travel website. After hearing it mentioned on one of those TV shows about people looking for vacation homes outside the states. She had searched the web and voila.

You know the shows I mean, right? Those are the ones you watch when you still have twenty five years to go on a thirty year mortgage and want to dream of having the resources to do what those people on TV are doing. Oh yeah, and it can be really demoralizing when the people doing the buying are all younger, more tanned and better looking than anyone in the TV audience!

But, this time Jane had done her homework. The owners were up on Facebook with a site for the place and she had read the homepage and the reviews. She had even connected with some of the people posting the reviews and from what they said, the place looked perfect for what she had in mind.

Jane was going to reinvigorate her marriage to Harry -- or she was going to end it. She knew Harry had no idea what she was thinking but she wasn't entirely sure he cared about her anymore. She wasn't sure of her place in his world and the insecurity was driving her crazy. It always seemed to be all about his factory these days.

She was just watching the calendar, biding her time and waiting anxiously. She really half expected him to beg off on the trip at the last minute and suggest she take one of her girlfriends instead. He had talked every night about the problems with the expansion at the factory and that irritated her. It irritated her because she could see no reason to squander the precious few hours they shared these days on work talk, unless he were building a case for backing out of the trip.

She knew intellectually, at least she hoped in her heart, that he still wanted to be alone with her and just spend time together. But she could also see clearly that he did not want to be "disconnected" from his factory. And, that is how Jane thought of it, "his factory." She often asked herself, why did he pay his department heads and assistants such high salaries if they were not able to run things and make sound decisions in his absence?

****

Meanwhile, Harry was finishing the phone call to his executive assistant but his mind was on his wife. He was worried. Sometimes Janie drove him crazy; and she always had. That was why she had attracted him in the first place. That was also why he now worked his butt off 12 to 14 hours a day in a thankless job running the business he had built from nothing after college.

As a college athlete, he had been good, real good, but he had not been great and there were no professional scouts waiting to talk to him and offer him deals when he graduated. No, that's not entirely true there had been a couple of scouts but in the end there were no serious offers. So, facing reality he set to work making a living and trying to give his family all the things he felt they deserved.

It was amazing how fast the time passed and the sequence of events that had brought them here today. There were bank loans and dental bills and doctor bills and mortgages he worried about. And there were payrolls to manage, and production schedules to meet, and taxes to pay, and more than he could handle some days.

Back at the beginning, their beginning, she would listen and he had liked talking to her about the challenges at work; but these days she seemed to lose interest and now he really wasn't sure some days why he worked so hard. It was like being a gerbil on the exercise wheel in the gerbil cage and he couldn't get off.

And, now she wanted to go to some crazy place in the Bahamas that wasn't even a resort because she had seen it on a TV show and then found it on the web. It was way the hell down some dirt road with no pool to lie beside and sun himself. Hell, he probably wouldn't even have a cell signal and there was no telling what shape he would find his factory in when he got back; right now he felt trapped, very trapped. They were booked on a flight a week away from now to Fort Lauderdale for a few nights at some marina resort for a few days.

Then they would fly on down to Eleuthera, wherever the hell that was! Well at least he could still check the status of things while they were in Florida. It was almost like she was trying to get him away from the factory. Maybe this was some kind of a test or something she had found in one of those women's magazines that she liked to read.

But right here right now, in the present, in the here and now, in his home, he needed to thank her for the sandwich. Then he needed to eat it and get back to the office as quickly as he could without tripping one her triggers. He told himself they were mostly happy and she had been a good wife and he told himself that he had been a good husband.

But he also realized there didn't seem to be any "magic" recently and there was definitely more tension lately and he knew it and she knew it. So, maybe this cottage on the beach idea was going to be a good thing after all. He knew they had somehow lost their way but he did not know how to find their way again and he did not know how to make things right again. That's what he did, he was a "fixer" in the corporate world and he always found a way to make things right. But this was different.

A week or so later the big day was here and Harry was trying to be patient but the car was coming to take them to the airport in less than an hour.

"Have you got your bag packed yet?" he yelled upstairs where Jane was feverishly throwing last minute items into her bag; actually it was into her bags, plural. She knew Harry would only have one bag and it would not be totally full while hers would be overflowing and she also knew he would not offer to reopen his to accommodate some of her last minute essentials.

Why was he like that she wondered, and if he was that damned organized why didn't he come upstairs and help her get ready for the trip? When had it started being her problem to get the bags ready alone? Well, OK, not "alone" maybe, but definitely without help.

Downstairs Harry knew exactly which pocket his passport was in and were his plane tickets were and exactly what was in each compartment of his travel bag; which true to form was only about two thirds full. He also knew she was just now throwing things into her bag that she might or might not want to see or use while they were in the Bahamas. Why was she like that?

She always waited until the last minute and then over packed. It would have been a simple matter to figure out what she was going to wear and then pack only those things. But, she wanted "options" so she waited until the last minute and then started throwing "options" into her bags.

****

But he wasn't going to give any excuse for another fight, not after the other day. Oh, no! All hell had broken lose when he said that if they had to do this, they could make it as quick as possible. So, Harry had proposed that they could make it all the way in one day arriving on the first day in the cottage. They would catch a flight from Atlanta to Ft Lauderdale in Florida and then make the connection from one terminal to another to find Silver Airlines. That way they could skip the resort in Ft Lauderdale and he could get some days back in his already busy life.

But Jane would have none of it and in the end Harry had apologized and said "OK." But this morning, by the time they got the bags into the back of the car for the airport they were already snipping at each other.

Luckily, although the lines were always long at Atlanta-Hartsfield airport, the place was set up to move people quickly and efficiently. They made it past check-in, through security and to the gate in plenty of time to board the flight and get comfortable in their seats. Then the metallic voice came over the airplane speaker system alerting the passengers to a mechanical problem that should be resolved momentarily and asked for their patience.

****

Jane just sighed and Harry's blood pressure went up about ten points. She knew better than to try to talk with him right now. She had seen this before. He was desperately trying to control something that he could not possibly control. He checked his I-phone looking for information on their connecting flight and half a dozen other things he could check looking for some way to get things back on track.

Finally, against her better judgment she said, "See, this is why we have the first few days at the Hilton resort hotel in Fort Lauderdale. We can just go there a little later that's all. Everything will still be OK." Jane smiled and it was almost working, then she added, "Imagine if we had been trying to make this all on one day!"

Why did she have to say that? Why couldn't she just let it go? Harry's blood pressure went up another ten points but he chose to ignore her comment, even though she could see that he took it as a jab at his proposed revision to her original plans. So they sat in silence in the stuffy cabin as another announcement told them that progress was being made and that the replacement part and the mechanic were on the way so the flight should leave within the hour.

And in order to expedite departure when all was repaired they would not be de-planning. The airline voice explained that it would take longer to de-plain and re-board the passengers, so the airline would start a quick beverage service for their comfort while they waited in the uncomfortable airline seats, on the plane, strapped in, the ground in Atlanta, trying to pretend everything was OK.

****

And, really it was OK. The plane did eventually take off and the flight was smooth. So what if they were a little later than planned, they had no appointments and no schedule for the next few days. And the cabin crew on the aircraft had gone out of their way to make everything as good as it could be, given the late departure. Jane was settling in for what she hoped would be a pleasant time together. Harry even appeared to have let his blood pressure drop a bit as he let himself relax and accept the reality and the inevitability of the situation.

****

An hour and a half later they lifted off and made their way to Fort Lauderdale. The flight was uneventful and the flight stewards did not skimp on the drinks so the general attitude in the cabin became better with a little time. By the time they touched down in Fort Lauderdale they were both actually smiling, seemingly without forcing it. Maybe there is hope after all, Jane thought to herself.

"I just hope the hotel transport is organized when we get there." Harry said almost to himself. It was the kind of comment that marked the uneasy peace between the two of them these days. For her part, Jane just kept hoping there would be some magic on Eleuthra that would turn this trip around. It was not turning into her dream vacation at this point but there was still hope.

That last statement summed it all up. Jane wanted to be carefree and maybe a little spontaneous at times and she had thought he was that way too. In fairness, she knew he would see it as planning for the worst case and always, always, always having a way to mitigate that worst case. But it came across to her as always looking at the glass half empty when clearly there was a lot of good in a glass half full - especially if it was half full of her favorite wine!

She just wasn't sure "he" was still her "favorite wine," and that was what this trip was all about from her perspective. Oh, she didn't have a love on the side and she was not trying to choose between Harry and someone else, she was trying to decide if Harry was the right future for her. So Jane kept smiling and Harry kept smiling and they both knew they were faking it.

4. JOHN & ERICA: WILLIAMSBURG IN THE REAR VIEW MIRROR

Meanwhile in Williamsburg, Virginia, Erica awoke in her apartment near the Law School at the College of William and Mary and stretched, luxuriating in the warmth of the sunlight streaming through the shades and feel of the soft sheets on the bed against her skin. She was making a good effort, and real progress she thought, to put the break-up with her ex-boyfriend, Brad, behind her; and John really was a good guy, and he was falling for her, she already knew that. She was just not quite ready to let herself love again so soon. "So soon? Really? It had been, what? About two years, entirely too long!" she told herself.

And yet she was also spending a lot of time, energy, and effort telling herself that it was not as serious with John as, she knew in her heart, it was becoming. This was not just a fling on the rebound, with a guy who wanted to take her to the Bahamas. This was clearly something different, but she was not yet sure exactly what it was.

****

John had awakened an hour earlier, before Erica had even thought about getting out of bed, and hit the gym for a workout and a run before his morning shower. He was a fit young man with a promising future as a junior banker at one of the bigger national firms that serviced the wealthy, semi-retired population of Williamsburg – and he was going places. He had admitted to himself that he also hoped Erica would consider going places with him.

He was hooked on her after their first cup of coffee

together. They had met at the W&M Bookstore coffee shop which was located upstairs in the front of the store looking out on the Duke of Gloucester Street and the shops of Merchants' Square. It had been a serendipitous meeting and just one of those things that happens when the time is right.

They were both oblivious to each other shopping for a child's book in the youth section of the store. She was looking for something for her niece, aged seven, and he was looking for something for his nephew who was six and a half. They had both reached for the same book at the same time. It was one of those chance meetings that you cannot script and cannot make up.

His hand was quicker and he got to the book an instant before she did. In fact she had actually wound up with his hand in hers reaching for the spine of the book. John deferred immediately to her and apologized handing the book over to her.

"She looked down at the book in her hand and said, "Maybe they have more than one copy."

"No," he said, "I already asked and came up here looking for it. But, I'll make you a deal." He added with a smile.

"What kind of deal?" she asked.

"Let me buy you a cup of coffee and the book is yours." And he gave her his best smile.

"Who could resist that?" she said and nodded, tucking the book under her arm. "Make mine a latte and grab us a table and I will go pay for this and be right back."

****

By the time she returned from the cash register he was placing two lattes on a little table in the front of the store by the rail looking out over Merchant's Square and the tourists migrating back and forth through the Colonial Area of the town.

She, he learned without too much prodding, was a graduate teaching assistant (GTA) in one of the programs at the college and often came to the bookstore for a cup of coffee. And he was just passing a little time on a day off wandering through the books on finance in the store and looking for a gift for his nephew.

He realized that she had known immediately he was not a student. Even in his casual clothes, he was better dressed than the general student population. And, as she had joked with him later, he wasn't wearing flip-flops.

He had laughed when she told him she thought it was one of the requirements for acceptance at William and Mary; that the students always wear flip-flops regardless of the temperature or weather conditions. Although, he had noted that they did at least wear long sleeve sweaters with their short pants in the middle of winter. That had been a delightful day for both of them.

****

Now, this moment in her apartment, she was in mid-stretch when she heard the door open and she knew John was back from his workout. She grabbed her backpack and threw it over one shoulder and stood there smiling at him as he came through the door.

"What are you up to, beautiful? Going someplace?" He asked her looking at the backpack and then letting his eyes travel down to her bare legs below the hem of her loose fitting sleep shirt. When his gaze hit her house shoes his smile broadened into a grin. "Let me clarify that, what are you doing? Is this a fashion statement or do you have some kinky side I haven't seen yet?"

"I'm, not telling," she teased, "you will have to find my kinky side all by yourself. But this," she indicated the backpack, "is what I plan to take as my bag, to the Bahamas."

John looked with incredulity at the medium sized backpack that Erica had slung over her shoulder, "That's it?! Is that all you have for the trip?" he asked.

Erica just smiled and said, "Couple of bathing suits, shorts and a couple of Tees, it is a beach right? An island surrounded by water, right? Why, what are you bringing?" as she eyed the backpack he had been packing last night and that now sat over in the corner of the room leaning against the wall.

John was't expecting that but he responded with a smile, "Shorts, trunks and Tees. And, yes, it is a beach and an island and I have cash, and my AMEX card and a spare toothbrush just in case." With that last he winked at her and reached for her backpack.

Erica blushed ever so slightly as she handed him her backpack and watched as he put it carefully against his in the corner. Then he came back and put his arms around her.

He felt good and somehow, she did not care that he had not yet showered after the gym. "You need a shower," she said not pulling away from him.

"I know." He said and then added, "Can you come and wash my back please?"

"Only if you wash mine too." She replied.

****

After the shower and the time in bed and the nap, they finished their packing and then enjoyed a little wine and cheese listening to soft jazz and went back to bed to sleep. The next morning they were up early and dressed for the trip to the airport.

As they walked out of her apartment, John grabbed both their bags in one big hand and put his other arm around her shoulders. This just might be a good trip she thought to herself as he led her to his jeep on the curb and put the bags on the back seat of the vehicle. They drove away from the curb listening to Jimmy Buffet and smiling.

Then as they approached the intersection of the Highway 199 bypass and Interstate 64 he turned earlier than she was expecting onto Highway 143. Obviously he noticed the question in her eyes because he immediately said, "I never use I-64 anymore! One idiot does something stupid and we go nowhere, and besides there has been construction off and on for 20 years and they don't seem to ever finish it. It is a 'jobs' program not an interstate!"

"But all those stoplights on 143?" She asked.

"All those stop lights mean that you can stop anytime you want to and get a cup of coffee and that is an option you do not have on I-64! Besides we will make it just fine, Newport News Airport is just not that far away." And he was right.

They were parking the Jeep within half an hour and with the backpacks as carry-ons, the check-in was painless. The flight they boarded was early to arrive at the gate in Fort Lauderdale and the hotel van was waiting for travelers headed to the Holiday Inn Marina Resort outside the airport. Everything just seemed to go their way. She was starting to see a pattern whenever she was out with him. Everything just went smoothly with no hassle and no complications!

****

5. ART & SAM: SETTLING IN

Art woke to the sound of a mosquito buzzing in his ear and when he stirred he saw Sam through the open door, standing on the porch, with a large beach towel wrapped around her shoulders but it did not completely cover her butt. She was listening to the sounds of the ocean and staring at the sun as it began to drop into the western sky off to the right side of the view from the porch. This time it was his turn to surprise her; at least he tried. But as he moved out onto the porch she just knew he was there and turned to press her body against his.

He just stood there in the fresh air feeling the breeze caress his skin and then he felt the tears from her eyes on his chest. He pulled her back to arms length and looked into her red eyes.

"You know I am never coming here again don't you?" Samantha asked in an emotional voice.

"Don't be silly," he chided her, "someone has to come back here hold my wake next year." Then he took a deep breath, said a little silent prayer, fortified himself and hoped it would spread to her, "But, Sam, this trip is about living and loving, so clean up your act and fix your face while I go get that last suitcase."

"You are putting on pants first, aren't you? Nude is OK on this side of the house by the beach." She said, adding, "People would just thing you are an over zealous sun-worshiper. But, on the other side of the house by the road you would just be an aging pervert. And," she continued before he could speak, "since we know people do drive by the backside on that road from time to time, I wouldn't want to spend the rest of the week trying to bail you out of the local jail." And, Sam was back to herself, and she smiled that thousand-watt smile in his direction and he fell in love with her all over again.

Art smiled back at her, still fastening the waistband of his trousers, and turned to head down the steep stairs for the last suitcase.

He was about half way down the steps when Sam lost it and the tears gushed from her eyes. He was so brave and so much a part of her life, and her very being, that it was tearing her apart as he tried to make this one last week together everything they had ever wanted together. This was important. It was important to her because it was important to him.

This would be the last time she would have this opportunity with Art because he was going to be gone soon – too soon. The thing, growing inside his body, would kill him within the year. He was dying. He knew it and she knew it and they were not going to even mention it. This trip was to be their chance to have one more great week together before going back home to the doctors who would make heroic efforts to save him but, in the end, the doctors would mostly preside over his demise.

****

As she heard him coming back up the stairs she ran into the bathroom and as he opened the back door in the little corner kitchen of the cottage. She flushed the toilet for effect, splashed water on her face, and came out patting her face dry with a washcloth.

Then as if nothing had happened she went to him and said, "Let me help you get that thing onto the bed so we can unpack it together."

Suddenly they were young again and this was just one more adventure. They had always packed together and unpacked together unlike some couples who had a "his" bag and a "hers" bag. Art joked that it was really the ultimate act of intimacy when your undies were comingled, and your toothbrushes were in the same travel case.

They put things away taking every opportunity that presented itself to look at each other, smile at each other and touch each other. By the time they finished the unpacking a glass of wine seemed like a really good idea and they sipped a cabernet while watching the sunbeams play on the water off the front porch of the cottage.

****

The next morning, Art rose early as was his custom and he rummaged around the kitchen to find an Italian style espresso maker in one of the drawers and in another he found some Bustelo espresso. He unscrewed the device into its parts and filled the water chamber and then the little metal basket with the fine ground black powdered espresso coffee. He screwed the thing back together and started to heat it on the stove.

Then he took two cups of milk and put them into the microwave. He waited patiently for the hot black liquid to start to drip over the internal spout of the coffee pot. And within minutes he was pouring hot espresso into hot milk and making a passable latte. He was feeling pretty proud of himself when he looked towards the bed and saw Sam lying elevated on one shoulder and one arm watching him. "You know the way to my heart!" she said with a groggy voice. Then

41

she swung her legs out from under the covers and sat up as he handed her the hot drink.

****

They walked out onto the porch to watch the sunrise. She wore her panties and he wore his shorts but it didn't matter because there was no one else around anyway. Then the chill morning air off the water made him realize that men have nipples too and he looked down to see hers stiffen and poke out much more pronounced that his. He stepped back inside and brought his shirt from the chair where it lay and draped it over her shoulders. Her smile thanked him. They just stayed there for a long while then she turned to him and said, "I think I smell rain."

He responded, "You're crazy! There is not a cloud in the sky."

"No dummy, sometimes you have all the subtlety of a rock! If it is going to rain then we have to come in to the porch and if it really does rain then we have to go inside the cottage. And once inside there is nothing to do except watch TV, or talk, or . . ." and her voice trailed off but he could see she was looking at the bed."

"Yes," he said putting his arms around her, "I believe I do smell rain . . ."

****

Later after taking turns in the little shower and dressing for the public, they got into the Jeep and headed back down the dirt road to the pavement and into the quaint little town of Governors Harbour. The late morning sun playing off the water illuminated the brightly colored houses along the bay in the middle of town. The little sail boats in the bay and the kids playing just made the scene complete. Art pulled the

Jeep into the parking area beside Da Perk, a cute little coffee shop open for breakfast and lunch only because the rest of the day the owners are enjoying the water and the beaches themselves.

Sam and Art sat outside at the rough square tables with brightly colored tops positioned on the deck in front of the little restaurant. The salt air and the sun partially shaded by an overhead trellis just made it a perfect setting. They ordered a couple of lattes and a couple of sandwiches and sat there just enjoying each other's company and the gorgeous weather for the better part of an hour. Finally, the time felt right to move on.

"So, what do you have in mind today?" Samantha asked Art.

"I thought we might drive north, if you are OK with that." He looked at her tentatively.

It always amazed her and in a small way touched her heart because he always, always, always wanted to get her agreement to things, as if her opinions really were the most important things in the world to him. So, she nodded enthusiastically and smiled encouragement and he continued.

"It is a little late in the morning and it is a long drive but I want to see Preacher's Cave if you are agreeable."

"Sure," she replied still smiling, "Sounds fun to go exploring. So what is Preacher's Cave and where is it?" Sam knew this was the cue he needed and he would talk for hours if she let him. And, today she might let him because the silence she knew was coming all too soon would be with her for the rest of her life.

****

Art started warming to the topic as they walked across the dirt parking area to the old Jeep. He opened the door for her and as she climbed in he put his hand on her butt to help her up and because they both enjoyed that intimate gesture. Then he went around to the driver's side and cranked the old engine to life. Two things happened; the car complained but started and some 1980's rock came across the car stereo system.

"Well, that's a surprise," he said with a big grin. On previous trips they had exhausted the few radio stations one could pick up in Eleuthra and none of them were clear nor did they have much music on them. "Where did that come from?" Art asked Sam as she sat there smiling in a self-satisfied sort of way.

"Well, I figured Jamison would find us a car that had a radio and a cassette player. I think this is the only place in the world where cassette players still exist. So, I found a cassette or two at a garage sale and have been hoarding them for months now, just waiting to see if they would work."

Just then the strains of **"Uga Chucka, Uga Chucka, I can't stop this feeling, deep inside of me, girl you just don't realize what you do to me!"** came through the car sound system and they sang along like a couple of kids. This was the music popular when they had first met and they knew the words to these songs and they sang them loudly for some miles.

The old music made a nice distraction from the occasional terror of driving on the wrong side of the road just like in the UK. That was bad enough but the act of doing that and meeting large dump trucks or school busses who had apparently decided to take their half of the road out of the middle was disconcerting to say the least.

Art eventually resumed his description of the cave. "Back in the mid-1600's a group known as The Eleuthran Adventurers set sail from Bermuda to escape religious persecution under the leadership of William Sayle. But apparently just being Puritans was not enough to ensure harmony and there was some dis-unity on the ships, which many think may have affected their ability to work together. The short version is that they shipwrecked on the reef known as the Devil's Backbone and managed to make it ashore alive."

This was the Art she had fallen love with. Here was the confident well-informed man who didn't seem to fear anything and who always researched the hell out of everything. Of course he had spent a career as an military officer and he had studied history at The Citadel down in Charleston, South Carolina, so it should not surprise her that he knew a lot about history and was constantly reading more.

All Art saw as he glanced over at her was a smile in her eye and on her lips so he continued. "Anyway, they made it to shore and found shelter in this enormous cave until they could start building what would become the first permanent English settlement in the Bahamas at Governor's Harbour."

"The larger ship was lost along with all the food and supplies but the seventy or so who survived did so by eating fruit and fish until they could get established. Along the way we will pass Glass Window Bridge and that may figure into this story too but I will save that part until we can see the bridge."

Sam agreed and turned the music back up and they

sang along some more as he occasionally reached over to touch her thigh, usually jerking his hand back to the wheel as another large truck would come careening along the road and then magically they would survive near death again.

****

Art and Samantha stopped briefly at Gregory Town for a little refreshment and to check out Pam's Island Made Gift Shop. This was once the center of the Pineapple trade in Eleuthra and the gift shop specialized in local crafts. Art and Sam joked that on these stops they were searching for things they did not need and could not live without. They always managed to find something they could not live without. This time it was candles that Samantha just had to have.

They left half an hour later heading north out of Gregory Town towards North Eleuthra, and eventually to James Bay to search for Preachers Cave. First though they had to transit Glass Window Bridge which is one of the most beautiful displays of the raw power of nature as well as one of the most dangerous places on earth. This is the narrowest part of the 110 mile long island and when the artist Winslow Homer painted the scene in the nineteenth century there was a natural rock formation that connected the landmasses with a sort of natural frame above the view provided by the opening in the rocks.

Viewed from the calm and peaceful Caribbean side one can see the emerald-green Bight of Eleuthra which is a calm body of water that seems to go on forever. The perspective then of the rock formation in the painting is as of a rugged frame around a glass window looking out onto a pounding, unpredictable surf caused by rogue waves out of the Atlantic Ocean. In fact the rock formation at the top of "the window" no longer exists and the top frame today is the latest in a series of bridges.

The current bridge was knocked eleven feet towards the Western side, the Bight of Eleuthra, by a rage on Halloween Day in 1991. Rage is what the locals call the phenomenon of huge waves resulting from storms far away in the Atlantic. As these waves roll towards the islands there is no barrier reef to slow or impede them. The natural rock face of the cliffs towering eighty feet or more above the Atlantic forces the waves like a sort of rock funnel. This funnel effect creates extremes of height and speed and power as they crash into the narrow crevice and throw up water with force a hundred feet or more into the air. The waves are forced against the narrow concave cliffs with the force to lift boulders the size of a small car.

So even on a clear sunny day these rages can erupt without warning to sweep away any and all on the bridge when they occur. There is no season and no cycle; just the raw power of nature exerting itself. Suddenly, Samantha wanted to rethink this whole excursion. As they approached the bridge, the height of the cliffs left them blind to the scene until actually entering the bridge. The Atlantic was heaving and rolling on the right and the Bight of Eleuthra was deceptively calm and serene on the left. She found herself urging Art to not spend too much time crossing the bridge as a forty foot wave broke below them under the right side of the bridge.

They both breathed easier, said a silent prayer and crossed themselves, when on the other side of the bridge.

****

On the return trip Sam could tell that Art was nearing the end of his reserves and she thought she saw him fighting sleep as he swerved just a little too much to avoid an oncoming truck. But she also knew it was important for him to be "the man" he always had been, so she didn't say anything or show any alarm on her part. What she did instead was an almost continuous stream of conversation. She told stories and reminded him of the good times they had shared and made comments about the countryside they were traversing. She kept him awake and alert and engaged as only a lover or a close friend can. By the time they got back he was tired but he was also more energized than he had been in a long time.

They made it back to the Pink Sand Cottage before the sunset and were able to enjoy that experience on the front porch with a glass of wine. Sam had turned her chair at an angle to his chair and placed her feet gently in his lap. Art held the glass with his right hand and massaged her feet with his left hand. He wasn't terribly good at massage and he knew it and she knew he knew it but what they really wanted was to touch each other's skin – just to feel the human warmth together.

The last rays of the sun disappeared along with the final drops of the wine. Sam stood, stretched and took his hand. Art allowed himself to be led into the bed and to fall asleep wrapped in each other's arms. He slept and she cried silently with the understanding that he would soon be gone.

****

6. ART & SAM: THEIR STORY

Samantha lay on the bed in the cottage, awake but not moving. She could see the waves outside, beyond the small deck. She listened to Art's breathing and his occasional soft snoring on the other side of the bed. The wind was warm coming through the open door and the open windows this morning and the sun was already above the horizon. The warmth felt good on her skin as she let her thoughts and her memories take over.

****

The two of them, Samantha and Arthur, had met and fallen in love relatively late in life. Both of them were veterans of the battle between the sexes and she had almost given up on her dreams when one day a little over thirty years ago he had just walked into her place of business. Perhaps remarkably, Samantha had not closed herself off to the potential of finding the right guy, like so many of her sisters had. She was fed up with the lies and the half-truths and the men who couldn't seem to make a commitment.

It was one of those guys who had most recently left his footprint on her heart. That man had been guilty of almost everything she hated but she had not known that at first. But she would learn all about it before their time together was over.

He had seemed like a regular guy. Just a regular guy who had never quite gotten around to getting serious. He had gotten around to being physical and he had gotten around to being very attentive. He had gotten around to seeing her almost every day and he had gotten around to long walks and affectionate evenings and weekends of near non-stop sex.

He had just never gotten around to defining a future for the two of them together or to making a commitment. Every time she had started to bring the subject up he became evasive and then she found out that he had gotten around to hitting on one of her friends. And he had gotten around to seeing other women from time to time on his business trips out of town. He had gotten around to almost everything except what she needed in a relationship. So she got rid of him and that's where she was in life when Arthur had walked into her café.

The café had been her anchor and her place to hide from the world when things went badly. It had also been her source of income and her one safe place from life's disappointments and life's pain. She was beginning to think she would be sitting in this café for the rest of her life and she was coming to grips with that and frankly she was starting to be OK with that. Then without warning, Art had walked in and she could still remember the day thirty years later like it was yesterday.

****

It had been a warm pleasant day just like all the others that summer. There was a morning rush of business people headed off to work, and then there would be a mid-morning push and then things would quiet down and she could relax a bit. That's when she would send her assistant to the bank or out to get supplies. It was on one of those days at that time of day and she was alone in the place. Then he walked in. There he was standing tall and straight and looking athletic and well dressed in uniform slacks and an open collared short sleeve shirt with some kind of insignia on

50

it.

He was rapidly approaching forty-something back then and she was in her mid-thirties. He had been a military officer who had come to the end of a twenty-plus-year career and she had finally turned her coffee shop and small custom bakery into a thriving business.

Samantha had been in the place alone when he walked in. Her helper was on a thirty-minute break and running some errands. Samantha smiled at him like she did to all new customers. Well, OK maybe a little more than she smiled at most new customers because he was kinda' cute. Then she had asked if she could help him from behind the safety of a cash register. He just stood there a minute, tall and fit and trim with a little grey at the temples in his Army uniform and asked if he could get a latté and her phone number.

"Excuse me." She had said non-committal and a little surprised.

"Well I think you are about twice as pretty as one woman ought to be and I don't see a ring on your finger. And, I don't believe in missing an opportunity to meet attractive interesting people, do you?" He said with a smile and a wink.

"How about I just get you that latte?" she replied. "Grab a seat and I'll bring it out to you."

He did as she had instructed placing his military hat on the table. She took her time filling the order and finally walked over carrying a small tray with two cups of coffee on it. She set the latte in front of him and a cup of steaming black coffee on the table as well. He did not say a word but gave her a slightly bemused look.

She pulled out the other chair and sat across from

him in the empty shop and sipped her coffee holding the cup with both hands and looking closely at him. He finally spoke, "Am I going to have to pay for two cups of coffee?"

"That's normally the way it works on a date, isn't it? The guy pays." She said as he burst into a smile as warm and friendly as she had ever seen.

"So, this is a date?" he asked.

"Actually it is an interview for a date." She said.

"How am I doing so far?" he asked playfully.

"I'll let you know in a few minutes," she said. "My name is Samantha but my friends call me Sam," she added.

"Hi, Sam. I'm Art, which is short for Arthur. I am a widower with a daughter away in college and I am planning to retire from the Army in just a few months. I own my car and my old truck and my bank and I have an ongoing relationship on the mortgage on my house. I am not shy and I think you are just about the prettiest girl I have ever not-quite-yet-met."

Sam smiled at that and replied, "I am coming off two, back-to-back, long term relationships and I do not want to be hurt again so I decided to start interviewing the guys before I date them. I own this business and my apartment and my car and a slightly used heart."

He looked thoughtful and took a sip of his latte. "So, how many guys have you interviewed like this?"

She took a sip from her own cup before answering, "Counting you, that would be one so far." They both smiled and sipped their drinks. He reached over and touched her hand as she set her cup down and she did not pull away.

It had started right there. Later when they knew

each other better they would often talk about it; about this moment; and about this touch. The touch was everything. From that moment on he wanted to only do one thing in life. He wanted to touch her skin. He needed to touch her skin, it was like a drug 'fix' and she had felt it too.

****

When her assistant came back to the café, she had looked over at the two middle-aged people alone in the shop with a quizzical expression on her face.

"Sarah," Sam said with a note of authority in her voice, "ring up a latté and a black coffee and give this gentleman the bill. Who knows he might even give you a tip."

The girl smiled, obviously confused but did as she was told. And, she was pleasantly surprised when the tall good looking man in uniform sitting with her boss threw down a twenty and told her in a soft low voice to keep the change. Then as Sam stood to leave his table and follow her assistant back behind the counter she slipped a folded piece of paper across the table to Art who quietly and quickly picked it up and glanced at the number. Then put it into his pocket. He called that evening and they had talked for almost an hour.

Now they had been together for almost thirty years. She still had that original coffee shop and a couple of more shops around the town, but she had sold her apartment and he had sold his house and they had moved into the suburbs together near a golf course. He had retired from the Army at Fort Jackson and started an insurance company with some of his buddies and it had grown into a successful local business in Columbia, South Carolina.

They were both successful in their careers and had enough money to travel when they wanted to travel, and they had "done Europe" as Art was fond of saying. He had been assigned many time to Europe in Germany and Italy and had travelled in France before they ever met. She knew he loved playing the part of the tour guide and she let him.

It had been fun and interesting and he did know a lot about the places they went. It was never as part of some pre-packaged tour with thirty people you had never met and would never see again. He took her places he knew well and shared them with her. His daughter had even joined a couple of times and she and Sam had gotten along well.

His daughter seemed to understand that Art needed someone in his life and she was fully accepting of Sam. The two of them could even bond on occasion and laugh about Art's personality quirks and share in a love of the man. But then the daughter grew as a woman in her own right and pursued other interests and her own career. And Sam and Art found Eleuthra and the cottage.

They were looking for someplace away from it all and without all the noise and glitz that comes with most vacation spots. This was it.

****

But here, now, as morning light was turning into broad daylight in Eleuthera, in the Pink Sand Cottage, on a sunny day, with the door wide open, the two of them lay spent from last night's activities in a tangle of arms and legs on top of the bed. He woke gently as he always did and rolled into her and smiled. They made love in a slow easy way and then lay there looking out at the tops of the palm trees swaying. She pulled a sheet over them on the bed as the breeze chilled her.

This was exactly why they had come back to this little cottage on this island. It was as if it were that very first day in her coffee shop. The feel of his skin unlocked some chemical deep in her brain or some need deep in her soul and she needed to feel his skin, his touch and his caress. He breathed deeply the scent of her hair as she lay with her head on his chest and he stroked her side and her back with the palm of his hand. He spoke first, "Baby, I just need to touch you. I can't get enough."

"I know, baby. I know." Was all she said as the breeze faded to a gentle caress of salt sea air mixed with that gentle sweet aroma that is the first smell of rain. They both drifted off again for a short nap.

****

She awoke to the smell of fresh coffee and he was moving around the tiny kitchen trying to be quiet. She sometimes wondered how he had survived all those wars he had been in and not learned to sneak up on anybody. He tried hard but he was not very quiet and she loved him for it.

She was vaguely aware that he had closed the door and closed the blinds so the mid-morning sun would not assault her senses too vigorously. Samantha stretched on the bed and felt more alive than she had in years. This was the man she had loved for half her life. Wow, it had in fact been almost exactly half her life!

Art was doing something that vaguely resembled preparing food. She remembered they had stopped at the little bakery on the street behind the Waters Store as they left with the supplies yesterday and bought two loaves of fresh bread. He had managed to mangle off some slices with a dull knife and toasted them in the oven and he was spreading butter on a couple of pieces and coconut oil on a couple more pieces of bread. And as she fully opened her eyes and focused there he was holding out a cup of coffee and a plate with the toasted bread on it.

Sam sat up gathering the sheets around herself and propping on a pillow behind her back. Art handed her the plate and cup of fresh coffee. Then he turned back to the kitchen to grab his own breakfast. He sat on the edge of the bed being careful not to topple her or her food in the process. Samantha held the cup in both hands and mouthed a quiet "thank you" to her husband.

"How did you sleep?" Art asked her.

"Uhmm, like a log." She smiled over the steaming brew, and continued, "Why do you ask, kind sir?" she added flirtatiously, "What might you have in mind?"

"Well," he leaned forward and kissed her cheek, "I have that in mind too; but first I thought we might drive out to some random tourist destination, have lunch and then just play it be ear."

"That actually sounds pretty good," she said. "Let me finish this coffee and grab a shower and we can go. OK?"

It didn't matter what they did, she was up for anything he wanted to do. This would be his last opportunity to control his life before the chemo treatments and radiation took away his strength in a vain heroic attempt to delay his death. He had a particularly aggressive and lethal cancer growing inside of him and they both knew how this would end. But right now he was alert and alive and vigorous – just like nothing was wrong and it inspired her to see him grab for every bit of life available to him one day at a time everyday. She knew what he was doing. He was doing his best to leave her with one last glorious memory here and now before he passed from this life.

****

Art went to the shower first and Samantha listened to the ocean outside the cottage through the open door. Right now it sounded like an angry sea today but this was not unusual in the morning on Eleuthera. This was not the gentle tide lapping at ones toes on a sandy beach they had experienced yesterday.

This was the eastern most island in the Bahamas and this was the Atlantic side where sometimes as high tide came in, it hammered and pounded in a relentless roar that never quite ended. Just as the powerful waves of water never quite ended and one more hit before the previous one had ebbed and flowed back to whence it came, the waves of sound never quite ended. As one was fading away another reached a crashing crescendo before the previous quite faded away.

This powerful show of force from the Atlantic Ocean is how the shells had been ground to sand and how this beach had gotten its distinctive pink tint so many eons ago. How fitting it was to be in this lovely place, the Pink Sand Cottage, so well named and in its innocence this place had given them many hours and days away from the world's intrusions into their life and their love together. But right now it was the reminder of the relentless waves that made her think once more of the thing living inside him that would take his life all too soon. It came in waves too and one wave of the cancerous evil never quite ended before the next

57

one came.

It was so like him to try to create something new and innocent and lovely from even this eventuality. She knew that Art wanted to give her one more memory to comfort her in his absence because that was their Pink Sand Cottage, their love, and their refuge that she could carry in her heart the rest of her life – and she cried silently as he showered.

****

A short time later he sat behind the wheel of the old jeep and she sat beside him as they took their life in their hands one more time and took off back up the twin ruts that would eventually join the paved road. Oh this wasn't the dangerous part, which would come in a few more miles. When they joined the main road they had nicknamed go fast highway during their first adventure on Eleuthra.

Theoretically, the driving was exactly opposite of the United States. Here they drove on the left and that could be a bit disconcerting all by itself. But, when you added the large dump trucks that always seemed to be in a hurry, and the local traffic that seemed not to be in a hurry, it was a challenge. And the tourists forgetting they should not drive on the right side of the road but the left side of the road, well things got a little more sporty.

Then of course there is the fact that not everybody drives on the left. In truth, everyone drove towards the center and moved to the left when approaching someone else. So, they both breathed a sigh of relief at the respite offered by a quick stop in town as they passed through. They pulled into the paved wide spot in the road that passed as a parking lot for the Waters

Store and found what they were looking for.

A few minutes later they had a bag with fresh bread, some cheese and a little ham to go with the bottles of water and beer chilling in the cooler in the back of the Jeep.

****

An hour later Arthur and Samantha were walking arm in arm along some random deserted beach on the Island. They really did not know where they were and really did not care. The important thing is they were together and touching. The touching was their drug and their addiction.

They felt the sand between their toes and the hard packed sand under foot. Sam leaned her head against his bicep from time to time as they walked. And at times he squeezed her shoulder with the arm that was draped over her shoulders. These were lovers' embraces and intimacies and they were worth everything to the two of them.

The beach was wide here, in fact it was unusually so, for Eleuthera. The craggy rocks to their left side rose above the dunes as if watching over them. To their right, as she looked at his profile it was framed by the sea that had calmed significantly as the day went on until it was a now gentle ebb and flow playing tag with their toes. They held hands and walked so close that she could smell his familiar smell mixed with the salt sea and the sand.

Sam leaned into his side and wrapped her arms around his long powerful left arm and rubbed her cheek against his bicep again in a loving embrace. Art reached across his body and placed his large right hand on her other shoulder and pull her even closer to him.

The movement ended in a long embrace on the beach in plain sight of anyone who might have been passing by.

The whole thing seemed all the more romantic because of the abandon with which it was done. Arthur inclined his head down and kissed her with all the feeling in his heart and the tears came into both their eyes. This would end way too soon.

"Sorry babe," Art said, "this has got be a trip to the islands without tears and I just failed! Thank you for all that we have. It is special and it is one of a kind in the world."

Sam squeezed him in reply and they stood there silently a moment longer then walked on silently holding hands and feeling the breeze on their faces dry the tears. The water reached their toes as the tide inched its way up the beach.

****

As they walked back she brought up the one thing that always put him in a good mood - their wedding. She always thought that was a bit odd since the wedding is supposed to be what the bride remembers, and she did remember it well. It was perhaps the happiest day of her life but he remembered it fondly too.

They were both Catholic, and she had never been married, and since he was a widower, there was no problem with getting the priest to perform the ceremony, complete with Mass and reception party afterward.

"Remember how handsome you looked in your dress uniform?" She asked as they walked hand in hand.

"I remember how beautiful you looked as you

60

walked down the aisle." He responded.

". . . And all your groomsmen in their uniforms. . ."

He interrupted, "And when you asked my daughter to be your maid of honor, I thought she was going to explode right there. . ."

"You know," Samantha interrupted him this time, "she told me you were way overdue for getting married. She had worried about you all those years after your first wife died and all those 'military women' as she called them who kept chasing you."

"No, they may have been checking me out but I was waiting for someone perfect, like you. Marriage has to be forever in my world and I am sure I will still be watching over you at every Mass you attend after I pass." She breathed easier now because she knew he was back in control and accepting his fate. He continued, "I think the Father was a little bothered when I told him we were not going to have the wake in Columbia, South Carolina but he seemed less perturbed when we assured him we would be using the niche in the columbarium for my ashes. I think he was afraid I was going to ask you spread my ashes to the four winds or something equally pagan."

"I know," Samantha said, "and you made the right decisions to use the niche. It won't go to waste. And if you don't mind waiting a bit I will someday be right there beside you." Their religious beliefs were a source of comfort for them in this time of crisis and they walked along for several minutes not speaking, just enjoying each other's company.

Arthur and Samantha were both firm in their beliefs and for a good Catholic, the Mass celebrated on Sunday around the world was just an extension of the

Mass and fellowship celebrated in heaven and they felt a connection that gave them comfort as they prepared for the inevitable.

But Art wasn't done yet. He was OK with leaving his ashes in an urn in the niche at the columbarium, but he insisted that Samantha come back to Eleuthra to St Paul's Catholic Church to hold the wake and the celebration of his life. Somehow to him that seemed appropriate so she had agreed.

****

7. HARRY & JANE: CHECKING IN

Harry and Jane did eventually get to the airport in Ft Lauderdale. There was a slight delay with the baggage claim but they did eventually get their bags and then made a dash out into the sweltering afternoon heat to look for the shuttle to the Marina-Hotel. They found the right spot to wait and the shuttle did come within about ten minutes and things were starting to look up but while the shuttle was air-conditioned, it seemed to stop at every possible stop at the airport to pick-up other hotel guests. The net result was that the inside of the vehicle was only barely cooler than outside. Harry got a little more distraught with every stop.

By the time the sweaty wilted group of passengers got to the hotel they were arriving along with two other shuttles as well as a cruise ship group who were all competing for attention at check-in. Jane could see that he was not having a good time. So as he continued to harrumph and fidget back and forth, she finally said to him, "Harry, why don't you go over to the business center and check on things back home. I can hold our place in line and the bellhop already has our bags."

"Good idea," he replied. He was trying to smile but she could see it was an effort and he wasted no time scooting over to the hotel's business center where he promptly inserted a credit card, logged onto a computer and started making phone calls. He was in his element and she could feel his blood pressure going down from where she was standing in line. She saw him tapping away on a computer keyboard and staring at screens as the images changed while talking on his cell phone and on a house telephone.

For her part, Jane was fine with the line and stood there smiling. She was more laid back anyway and right now she was happy just to be closer to their holiday. One of the barmaids came over carrying a tray and offered her a glass of something clear, bubbly and tasty with a vague hint of alcohol. "Hmm, now that's good!" She said to the girl.

"Well, you looked like you could use one. Think of it as the manager's way of apologizing for the delay getting you all checked in." The young waitress said to her and smiled back at Jane.

"Can you do me a favor?" Jane asked.

"Sure, dear, what do you need?" the waitress asked in that ultra friendly way that barmen and waitresses have of talking to customers. And yet, nobody seems to mind the familiar tone of their voices.

Jane looked asked, "Can you take one of these to him?" and she pointed to Harry sitting with a phone in to his ear balanced on his shoulder and typing away still on the computer keyboard.

"I don't know," she said, "He looks pretty busy and maybe a little grumpy." She added with a grin and a little laugh.

"I know," Jane said, "You're right on both counts but I'm his wife and I'm hoping this will help cheer him up. And here's ten bucks for your trouble."

The barmaid waived away the bill and headed towards Harry. She stood in front of him for just a moment than spoke to him and Sandra could faintly hear something about, ". . . the pretty lady in line . . ." As she held it out and Harry took it with one huge hairy hand.

Then something happened. Harry smiled and took a sip. He smiled again, then said to the phone, "OK guys, I got what I need, keep up the good work. I gotta' go." And, he did. Harry hung up the phone, retrieved his credit card and picked up the long stemmed glass full of effervescent liquid.

He walked across the crowded lobby smiling and sipping the cocktail and made his way to Jane, "She said the pretty lady in line sent it over. So I looked over and the only pretty lady I saw was you. I came to thank you."

Sandra lifted up on her toes and kissed his cheek, "You just did." She said.

****

They were in the line for only a couple of more sips when their turn came with registration. The desk clerk put their data into the computer screen and then said apologetically, "There seems to be a problem. The room for which you were scheduled is still occupied. Some other patrons have been held over because their cruise ship has been delayed a couple of days."

Jane spoke up before Harry could get spun up, "So, can you do anything for us?" She asked with her best smile.

"Of course," the desk clerk said as he waived his supervisor over. The two men stood there looking at the screen and pointing at different things. Then the supervisor walked away and the younger man said, "You only need a few days so we are going to put you into one of our DV suites, if that is ok?"

"You're upgrading us?" Harry said incredulously.

"Yes, of course, besides you and your lady seem to already be in the mood of things with the drinks. And, you have waited so patiently, and you are both smiling, so we think you deserve an upgrade!" He said as he handed over the electronic key card to Jane.

To Harry he said, "Just show the bellman which bags are yours and he will bring them up. You will be in this building with a view down towards the Marina courtyard pool and marina bar; which I might add, has excellent Mahi-mahi. And a pretty good wine selection."

Jane noted that Harry was smiling, really smiling for the first time all day. She took his arm and leaned against his shoulder for a couple of steps. He responded by leaning down and kissing her briefly on the lips - and in public. This was turning out to be a pretty good day after all.

****

They made it upstairs, left the bags, then made it down to the outside bar in time for a little food. Jane ordered the conch fritters with a salad and Harry had the Mahi-mahi, which was very good, and a good glass of wine. The food came quickly and they relaxed throughout the meal; a little ore with each bite.

This began to feel like the vacation she had planned and hoped for. Harry and Jane talked and made plans like they had done at the beginning back when they were young. Then the unusual happened, Harry ordered a second glass of wine and they just sat there and talked.

Harry seemed to be in no hurry to pay the bill and Jane was enjoying the night air and the music combo playing by the pool was really quite good. She looked around and took in the couples flirting with each other at the open air bar, and she was enjoying the sound of

Harry's voice talking to her for a change and not at his phone. The second glass of wine came and they toasted and chatted until she was totally at ease and smiling with her eyes and not just with her lips.

Then he paid the bill and they went upstairs to continue chatting until they made love. Somehow it did not seem forced at all. In fact it seemed like the next logical and most natural thing in the world to do. And, they slept until the sun woke them.

Day Two For Harry And Jane

The sun that came streaming into the room through the open curtains made Harry open his eyes. Instinctively, he reached a sleepy hand over to Jane's side of the bed but she wasn't there. He sat up momentarily disoriented but smiled as she came out of the bathroom. She was wearing a bathing suit with a pink cover-up over the swimsuit and a pair of sandals that showed off her pedicure. She came over to his side of the bed, bent down and gave him a kiss on the cheek.

Harry responded by reaching up for her but she evaded his grasp, "Uh-uh, she said playfully. There is sun to be soaked up and I need a cup of coffee. Why don't you clean yourself up then go to the business center and check on the factory. When you finish at the business center you can come out and buy me breakfast. Don't be too long though, I do look pretty good in this outfit and somebody else might come along."

"Yes ma'am, that sounds good to me," he said smiling, "well except for the part about someone else buying you breakfast. That's my job! Otherwise, you got yourself a deal."

It pleased him that she was thinking about the importance of the factory to him personally and to their future. He decided right there that he would indeed check on things this morning but it would be brief. "Give me twenty minutes to shave and shower and maybe another ten in the business center. I will be there in half an hour!" Harry promised.

"I'll hold you to that." Jane said as she walked to the door and left the room.

****

It was more like forty-five minutes by the time he joined her but he was still smiling so she smiled back. They found a table in the shade and she moved there with him. The waiter came over quickly and they ordered a light breakfast with some fresh fruit and a couple of latte' coffees.

"How are things back at the office?" She asked.

"Surprisingly good." He responded smiling, "That new management team is starting to talk to each other and I didn't have much to do this morning during the conference call. A couple of more days like this and I will be a lot more comfortable leaving the expansion for them to worry with. But, how was your morning?"

"Well I had a glass of juice waiting and took a little stroll into the gift shop looking for some small things I can use as gifts. Then I found the clothing shop at the end of the hall, but the prices are outlandish . . ."

Harry thought how nice it was to just hear her talk, about nothing really just the sound of her voice was enough for him. It was like things were a decade ago and he was enjoying it immensely, then suddenly he realized he was expected to say something.

" . . . so, what do you think?" Jane asked again.

"I think you are beautiful and I was just enjoying the sound of your voice." Harry said.

"So, you quit listening?" she said with some indignation.

"No, baby, I was just listening to the music in my heart." Harry tried again and this time she smiled, a real smile that showed a dimple on one side. "But if you repeat the question, I can assure you that the answer will be 'yes, of course, whatever you want' because this is our vacation and our chance for some time together. So what was the question?"

"It doesn't matter." Jane said now really smiling. "Let's take a walk and hold hands like we used to."

Harry signed the check for the breakfast; then stood, pulled her chair out and put his arm around her shoulder as they strolled slowly away from the table. They followed the same path she had walked earlier and sure enough the prices in the stores were still outrageous. So instead of shopping they went for a dip in the pool and lay in the sun a while.

Jane was enjoying this and it seemed she had a different spf-rated suntan lotion for every part of her body. Harry didn't use anything and started to burn fairly quickly. When he finally realized he was turning pink he moved under the shade of a palm tree on her other side.

She lay there soaking up the sun and sipping some sort of bubbly water with a piece of fresh fruit in it. For his part Harry sat sipping a cold beer and picking from a cup of bar nuts the waiter had brought with the beer. And, he enjoyed looking at Jane and just talking.

Eventually she took pity on him and suggested they move into the air-conditioned lounge for a bite of lunch.

Harry couldn't agree fast enough. The cool air felt good and the food was superb.

****

After lunch they went up to the room for a quick shower and then found a hotel shuttle that would drop them in one of the local shopping districts. Harry tipped the driver and Jane found some little specialty shops that were much more reasonably priced and did the little shopping she had to do. Harry paid the bills and carried the bags and loved every minute of it. They lost track of time, and that was OK.

Finally they decided to eat a meal away from the hotel and found a local restaurant that was not part of a national chain. By the time they grabbed a taxi back to the hotel they were holding hands and almost snuggling in the back of the taxi.

Arriving back at the hotel the doorman just smiled and ushered them in. Jane noticed that Harry did not go to the business center to check on things and that his arm was around her shoulders as they went up to their floor in the elevator.

They made love that night in an unhurried and almost gentle way that long time lovers sometimes do, with a warmth and understanding of each other that defies words. And Jane slept well.

Day Three for Harry And Jane

The sun came beaming in through the sheer curtains in an explosion of light that woke Jane early and this time it was she who reached for Harry and did not find him there beside her. She listened but did not hear the shower or the sound of his electric razor coming from the bathroom.

She lay there a minute thinking through where he might have gone and was on the verge of being a little peeved, when he carefully opened the door pushing it with his foot. He walked in awkwardly carrying two large lattes and a small bag of something that smelled good.

"I had hoped to get back before you woke." He said apologetically.

"If that bag has some of those butter croissants from the coffee shop downstairs, you are forgiven for everything you have ever done or thought about doing." Jane said running her fingers through her hair trying to give at least some order to it without getting out of bed.

Harry smiled and set the cups and the bag of croissants on her night stand and leaned over and kissed her lightly then handed her one of the coffees. He sat on the side of the bed and they ate and chatted and laughed like they had done when they were dating so long ago. And eventually she got out of bed and went to shower and dress while he went down to check in at the business center.

Jane was very happy however when she came down to find that he had in fact finished his calls quickly and was sitting with a newspaper waiting for her in the lobby. As she approached, he put the paper down and stood to greet her. "What would you like to do today?" He asked her.

"I don't know," she replied, "any ideas? It's cloudy and looks like it might rain today."

"Well, actually I do," he replied, "I have two all day passes to the water taxi which will allow us to sightsee and get on and off as we like." Jane nodded her approval, and he continued, "And this afternoon I thought we might catch the mermaid show at the old Yankee Clipper Hotel. They have portholes all around that look out into the pools around the bar with girls dressed as mermaids for entertainment. The place is now called the Wreck Bar or something like that and the area has become the 'B Ocean Resort' but it was a real hotspot in the 1960s according to the brochures at the concierge desk."

"Sounds good," Jane said. "Did you check on things at home? Everything OK?"

"No." Harry said simply. "I pay them a lot of money to make the right decisions and they need to do exactly that."

Jane stopped dead in her tracks. "You're serious?" She said.

"Yes, I am serious. I might have made one little short phone call, but it was less than five minutes. The rest of the time was coming up with these activities. How am I doing?"

"Harry, baby, you have come a long way in three days and you are doing just great!" And she meant it.

****

The day was unscripted, loosely planned and a lot of fun for both of them. They even found time to wander through one of the biggest flea markets they had seen and just walked around looking at things and holding hands.

Harry and Jane did find their way to the Wreck Bar in time for the mermaid show and they did the "tourist thing" by riding the elevator up to poolside where the mermaids would chat and pose with the guests for pictures. It was corny and a little touristy but they did it

and enjoyed it and laughed the whole time.
****

That night when they got back to the hotel room, Jane was the one to hang out a do not disturb sign and push the door closed then secure it with the chain. Then she pulled Harry close, started unbuttoning his shirt and then his belt while he just stood there enjoying her touch.

They made love several times and it was hot and hard and satisfying and they slept in each other's arms.

Harry and Jane Day Four - Travel Day

The next day at mid morning they checked out of the hotel and took a shuttle back to the airport to the terminal where Silver Airlines operated. Once inside, finding the counter was easy enough and it was manned with a cooperative ticket agent who did expedite their check-in and point them towards security. Taking the escalator at the end of the terminal up to security went well despite a relatively slow line. They made it to their aircraft with time to spare and were strapping in as the pilot started the engines.
****

The plane was a twin engine turboprop and it had a low ceiling that gave it a definite claustrophobic feel. Nevertheless, Harry managed to get a seatbelt around his midsection just as the flight steward walked back and asked if they could please move to another seat so they could balance the load inside the cabin to compensate for the way the luggage was loaded.

Harry looked at the flight steward incredulously, "Are you serious?" he asked.

"Yes, sir. Can you please move back a few rows to help us balance the plane?"

Jane watched as Harry's blood pressure went back up a few notches. Maybe it was not at its previous high but it definitely went up a bit. Harry unbuckled his seatbelt and moved back a few rows with all the grace of a walrus. All the while Harry was mumbling to himself about incompetence and amateur hour airlines. Then he sat quietly and fumed looking at the back of Jane's head several rows further up.

****

Mercifully, the flight was short even if the plane was noisy and cramped. They bumped to a stop and Harry made his way up the aisle to where Jane was waiting. He forced a smile and gestured for her to precede him out of the plane. He gathered their luggage and they dragged the bags across the tarmac to the shoddy looking tin roofed commercial facility that greeted them.

A tall black lady smiled an easy smile but firmly asked Harry and Sandra to remain on their side of the red painted line on the cement floor. "This is the limit of the immigration line," she explained.

This American man, who she had heard his wife call Harry, might be surly but Sunny had been working at the Governor's Harbour Airport a long time and she did not take the bait. She had been doing this too long to confuse tired travelers with really grumpy people. After all, she thought, the tired travelers will be friendly once they rest and the grumpy people will still be grumpy when they leave this paradise. And that would be their punishment; they would have to leave paradise. Sunny smiled to herself.

And, she and her sister, Sweetness, and her husband, Jamison Smith would have something to discuss in the evening in the house they shared down on the beach before Sunny and Jamison went upstairs for bed. Sunny knew this so she took Harry's passport with a non-committal look on her face but gave a real smile for the lady as she handed her passport back to her. After all, Sunny reasoned, this pretty lady had to put up with Harry, no point in adding to her burden with a frown.

That was pretty much the same way Sweetness saw things and she handled Harry and Jane as just one more tired couple trying to clear customs. Sweetness did however note that Jamison had not come in yet to help with their bags until she had made her decision so he was not sure yet either.

She could see him through the outer door on the curb with that nice older couple who had just arrived on the island a couple of weeks ago. Now they were outside with Jamison to return their rental car in preparation for departure. Oh well, she thought, we will see.

****

While all of this was going on inside at the customs and immigration stations, quite a different drama was presenting itself outside on the curb. Art and Sam pulled up to the lot beside the international terminal at Eleuthra and parked beside the tin roofed building that housed the International Arrivals facilities. There was Jamison, waiting patiently for them.

"Jamison," Art said, "thank you for waiting."

"Yes," Samantha chimed it, "thank you so much for the extra time with the car. It meant a lot to us."

75

"No problem, man." Jamison took the keys and helped them with the bags. And, as he walked with them, "The other couple who have reserved this car are late due to delays in their connection. In fact they just arrived on the plane that will take you home. Your timing is perfect."

Sam thought to herself with a little bitterness, "Take us home indeed! What that plane is taking us to is the end of our lives as we have known them." But, she wiped the tear from the corner of her eye and forced a hundred watt smile. After all Jamison did not know any of this, so aloud she said, "Well, hopefully they are a nice couple. Do you know them?"

"No, Mrs. Sam. This is their first time on Eleuthra, so who knows? They may adapt and adjust or they may just hit their heads against the wall for a couple of weeks. We will see."

Sam hugged Jamison, "Well, we better go inside and get checked-in. You take care of yourself, Jamison."

"Yes ma'am." He responded as he took Art's outstretched hand and gave the firm handshake of men who understood how the world works. Art and Samantha walked twenty feet and disappeared into the International Departures area of the building just as Jamison turned to greet Harry and Jane as they came out of the door.

****

"Mr. Harry? Mrs. Jane?" Jamison asked with a smile in his voice."

"Yeah." Harry answered. "You the rental car guy?"

"Yes. I'm Jamison and your car is ready." He handed the keys to Harry.

Harry took a quick glance at the car and made a comment about the scratches on the car.

Jamison asked them, "Where exactly are you going?"

"A place called Pink Sand Cottage, do you know it?" Jane asked.

"Yes, I do, so you will see there will be even more little scratches on the car when you bring it back. And, on that road you will need the Jeep, trust me man." Jamison said by way of answering Harry's complaints about the car. Then he gave directions on how to find the cottage but Harry was not really listening and Jane was only half listening as she fiddled with something in one of her bags. So it was not surprising that they were lost almost before they got out of the airport.

Harry and Jane wandered around lost for a while and only managed to find the way to their destination at dusk, leaving the pavement and heading down the dirt road to the cottage. They spent a miserable night falling asleep with the bags only half unpacked and their clothes in disarray everywhere with no room left for anything resembling order. They fell asleep watching the little TV screen up in the corner of the room with the air conditioner running and no sound of the ocean and no breeze and no smell of rain.

****

8. JOHN & ERICA: AT THE MARINA

John and Erica meanwhile had raised a few of eyebrows when they arrived at the Hilton Marina Hotel in Fort Lauderdale with two backpacks and no other luggage, and they were clearly enjoying each other's company. But the hotel staff had seen young people in love before and, while knowing glances were shared among the staff, nothing was said to the young couple.

John and Erica went up to their room, threw their backpacks onto the bed, came back down to the lobby and headed outside to the bar. They both ordered beer in frosty mugs and he tried the fish tacos while she ordered a salad with chicken breast on top. They sat sipping their beer enjoying the warmth of the day and chatting. Their flights had been on time and there had been no problems getting here. They were even the last pick-up on the shuttle bus route at the airport and that had been a straight shot here.

When the food came they ate with gusto and then returned to the room and fell asleep in each others arms. John held her while she slept and was at peace with the world. He could see that Erica was tired and probably a little unsure of where this new relationship of theirs was going and, for his part, he was willing to just hold her and comfort her and wait for her to catch up to him.

In the quiet moments, he prayed she would in fact catch up to where he was in the relationship. He felt this was the one true love he might find in this lifetime. He just couldn't tell her that yet.

****

John was up early and the sound of the shower woke Erica, though she lay there pretending to still be asleep. As he got dressed he came over to her and kissed her forehead. "You're cute but you're not fooling anyone! I know you are awake," he said, "but I am going down to check out the yachts along the dockside here at the Marina."

At least that is what he said, but Erica knew he was just giving her a little space and a little alone time. As if reading her mind, before he left the room he suggested she meet him in about an hour for breakfast and some sun and fresh air.

She spent the time alone in the room getting ready at her own pace and thinking about everything. John had surprised her, because somehow in the back of her mind she thought bankers were supposed to be stuffy and a little cold. But John was none of those things; if anything he was the exact opposite. He had shown her nothing but warmth and understanding and he had been careful not to push. And, he was careful to give her the space she needed to sort out her thoughts. "Careful," she thought, "being around John could be habit forming!"

****

As John started exploring he took his time. He stopped in the coffee shop in the lobby and studied the menu as they prepared his latte. Then he sipped the drink while he strolled down the wooden path to the end of and the dock and back. And then he continued in the other direction, occasionally waving to the occupants of the yachts, and winking at one lady in a bikini who was posing by the rail of a very large cruiser. He even stopped and chatted with the owner of one of the smaller boats for a while.

In all he spent a very pleasant forty five minutes

and got back to the coffee shop just before Erica arrived. John ordered two lattes, his second and her first, and a fruit plate as well as a plate of sliced meats and cheeses that looked good in the picture on the menu. Erica strolled over to the table where John was sitting, arriving with the lattes.

John smiled up at Erica and as he stood for her he said, "Baby your timing is impeccable." John stepped around the table and pulled out her chair while the waiter put the lattes on the table.

Erica wore a two piece swim suit with some kind of cover-up over the swimsuit. The red nails of her pedicure set off nicely against the white sandals and her dark sunglasses under a big, wide-brimmed hat finished off her outfit. John thought she was the most beautiful woman he had ever seen and said so, "Erica, you look like a million dollars, trust me I'm a banker, I know what a million dollars looks like!"

Erica actually blushed at his comment, she wasn't sure why, she just did. She had been complemented before on her looks and she had always tried to look the best she could but somehow she really liked hearing it from him.

She knew she looked "put together" but to him she looked like the rest of his life and he wanted to tell her so, but he did not want to scare her away. She paused just a second in front of the table and then sat. It was so typical of John to have ordered her coffee and timed it to be there just as she walked in and then give her credit for the timing. He really had an uncanny sense of things.

"You look awesome!" he said unashamedly and before she could respond he continued, "I have taken the liberty of ordering a couple of plates we can share if you like." As if on cue a waitress appeared with the two platters and placed them on the table in front of and between the two of them.

Erica gave a little laugh, almost like a little girl, indicating her obvious appreciation of the platters and the coffee. As she reached for a small piece of the Italian salami and a piece of the cheese, she felt her stomach rumble. She must be hungrier than she realized, she thought.

And with that they settled in for a long leisurely breakfast just enjoying the conversation and each other's company. They both seemed to appreciate the gift to the senses of the good food and the warm sun streaming in through the floor to ceiling windows. They talked about everything and about nothing; and they laughed. They laughed often and openly. The laughter came from somewhere down deep and it warmed her to the core. She sipped her latte and looked at him seeing him in a different light and seeing a greater depth to him than she imagined bankers had.

He took the last swallow of his latte and he looked at her. "So, Erica, what do you want to do today? Is there some place you want to go, or some thing you want to see?"

"Yes," she said brightly and immediately, "I want to go shopping."

"Shopping?" John questioned. Then added with a note of affirmation in his voice, "Then shopping it is!" and he stood to hold her chair and they walked away from the coffee shop hand in hand.

"But a little detour first." She said as she led him outside to where the boats were parked. She just wanted to walk slowly beside him and smell the sea air and feel the sun for another few minutes.

"OK. Whatever you want." He said with another little smile.

She wanted to tell him that she wanted to go shopping because he was with her and she had not felt this way for a long, long while. She wanted to explain to John that it was not the amount of stuff she wanted to buy or the money she wanted to spend. She wanted to go shopping for a memory.

She did not know how to explain so she stayed quiet and just enjoyed the touch of his hand. Besides, would he even "get it" about her. She wanted to go shopping for some little thing. Maybe a pair of earrings or a scarf or even some tourist trinket. She wanted to get something that every time she saw it, or smelled it, or touched it, or put it on, that it would remind her of this day and this moment with this man in this place.

Erica pulled down on his hand and he moved closer and she wrapped both arms around him and hugged him on the boardwalk in the warm light of day among the other couples and tourists and boat owners at the Marina Hotel.

****

He teased her all the way to the shopping district in the taxi. "You are traveling to an island with everything for the trip in a backpack. What are you going to buy and where are you gong to put it?"

She answered immediately, "I am going to put it in your backpack, of course!"

That stopped him for just a minute as he tried to think of something to say.

****

Later they were in a part of town he never would have gone to on his own with little shops and cafes and sidewalk restaurants. How had she known this place existed. When they had asked the concierge about shopping he had suggested half a dozen paces and she chose this one off the list.

In any event, she found what she was looking for in the third shop they entered. It was a scarf of bright colors that seemed to blend into each other. The yellow and the peach and orange and a touch of red seemed to be part of one bright swirl. He could see that she liked it a lot and he reached for his wallet while asking how much it was.

"Oh, no!" she said firmly, "This is my memory, I will pay for it." And, with that she pulled a charge card from her jeans pocket and handed it over to the sales clerk.

John just smiled indulgently and offered to carry the bag when her transaction was done. He had noticed a coffee shop and asked if she would like to join him in a cup. She nodded enthusiastically and they walked hand-in-hand across the street to the coffee shop.

****

That evening after they had eaten and again taken a leisurely stroll around the docks of the Marina he sat on the little deck off the side of the room where they had a secluded view of the water and sipped a beer. She excused herself for a few minutes and he spent his time thinking about the day and how well everything had gone. He thanked his guardian angel for leading him to her and began to consider what a long term relationship might be like.

His reverie was interrupted when she killed the

light in the room and then stepped through the doorway, walked around him with her back to the water and leaned against the rail directly in front of him. The moon highlighted her form in the near darkness but he could see she was wearing the scarf, from this morning, tied over one hip and draped around her waist. Erica was wearing the scarf and nothing else. Stray moonbeams sneaked through the scarf between her legs and he could see the outline of her through the shear material of the scarf. John was dumbfounded and couldn't bring himself to speak so he just looked at her in the moonlight.

****

Finally she spoke, "Now, I think, this scarf will be a memory for you also." She said. "Every time you see it on me you will think about this night, and every time you see another woman wearing something similar you will think of me."

"This is what I was trying to explain earlier, I like little things that remind me of people and sometimes places. Today I bought a new memory and now that you understand, it will be something we share. This is our memory and I will think about it every time I see this scarf in my drawer and for certain every time I pick an outfit to wear it with."

John stood wrapped his arms around her and hugged her close as he whispered into her ear "Thank you. I understand now. We are building memories." He led her into the room without another word and closed the balcony door and pulled the drapes. And, alone in the room together they built another memory.

****

John and Erica spent two more days together at the

Hilton Marina Hotel and every one of them was better than the one before. Finally the day came for their reservation in Bahamas and they took the shuttle back to the airport and found the counter for Silver Airlines.

It was an easy flight, and upon landing they grabbed their backpacks and walked across the Tarmac to the metal building that served as international arrivals at Governor's Harbour on the Island of Eleuthra, Bahamas. At immigration, a tall good looking black woman noticed the different names on the documents and said, "Young lady, are you traveling under your own free will, or have you been coerced?" and then she turned a stern gaze at John.

"Excuse me?" Erica said, then recovering her composure despite the warmth of a blush she felt creeping up her cheeks, she quickly added, "Yes! Absolutely, everything is good here." And, with that declaration she reached both arms around one of John's muscular arms which stretched the sleeve of the T-shirt he was wearing.

"Well, as long as you are sure . . ." The tall, stern official looking woman said. Then she waived them across the red line painted on the floor and winked at Erica as the couple stepped to the next station to clear customs.

There was another attractive black woman who was obviously related to the first one, standing there behind her counter with her arms folded. Then her face broke into an infectious smile as she said, "She shouldn't do that but she likes to tease people and you look like a fun couple."

"What?" John asked in confusion.

"Well my sister likes to tease people and you two

show up with no baggage except the backpacks. You are both young and attractive and probably have different last names, so she decided to have a little fun at your expense."

At this they both breathed easier and the second woman continued, "There is no problem here. With just the two backpacks I am pretty sure you are not smuggling television sets or drugs to sell." Then turning to a tall athletic looking black man the customs woman said, "Hey Jamison, this lovely couple is waiting, so give them a good car, OK?". Then back to the couple, "And, you two, have a nice day and enjoy your visit to our island."

Jamison opened the door and ushered Erica and John outside as he suggested they step over to the local bar across the parking lot and have a cup of coffee. He explained that his most reliable car was coming back in a matter of minutes and he would love to buy them a coffee while they waited. The three of them talked about the Island and the previous trip that John had made here and how this was Erica's first time in Eleuthra. Jamison recommended some other locations they might want to visit and the whole experience was very positive for them.

Erica reflected that everything went so smoothly when she was with John and everything was fun, this could be habit forming, she thought to herself and smiled. He really did have an uncanny sense of timing or so it seemed when she was with him. Then it hit her, he was thinking everything through very, very carefully

Now that was flattering, she thought. Not only was he attentive at a level that she could see but he was clearly attentive at a whole different level that she had never experienced in a lover before. He planed for her having a pleasant time in everything they did together. Wow! She thought, I better be careful with this one or I will be his forever.

****

9. REGGIE & ALICIA: OPPOSITES ATTRACT

United States Air Force Staff Sergeant Reggie Smith, born in South Carolina, had spent his summers growing up working and on his grandfather's tobacco farm. Those summers had been hot and steamy and the work was hard and dirty and sweaty. That experience more than any other single thing had been his primary motivation to join the Air Force and "see the world" as the recruiters had said.

He wanted out of South Carolina and he wanted out of the family tobacco business. So the Air Force seemed like a pretty good deal and it had worked out pretty well. So far he had seen Germany and Italy and then he saw Maxwell Air Force Base in Montgomery, Alabama. That was three years ago and he was so glad to have come here he thanked his guardian angels everyday and said a little prayer for them. He meant it too!

Montgomery, Alabama was also where he had really learned about the Auburn-Bama football rivalry. See, this was not like some little Clemson versus the University of South Carolina rivalry. Oh no! This was a real rivalry. This was a feel it down deep in your gut rivalry. And since Auburn was about forty five minutes drive up the interstate from Montgomery he had seen some really good football games.

And a couple of times he and his buddies had pooled their resources and made the drive to Tuscaloosa to watch some games at the University of Alabama. It was just not possible to live in this state and not pick one side or the other. They almost forced you into it!

Reggie often told the new guys about his experience signing the contract for an apartment in Montgomery.

At the closing after the manager had made a copy of his I.D. card and run his credit check and Reggie was about to write the first check, the apartment manager asked a question. "I'm sorry, young man, I didn't ask you whether you favor Bama or Auburn?"

"Well, sir, I don't really follow college ball . . ."

The manager cut him off, and looked at him as if he had grown a third eye in the middle of his forehead. Then the manager said, "I'm sorry, was that Bama or Auburn?"

Reggie realized he was going to have to make a choice right then an there, so he flipped a mental coin and said, "Bama, sir, Roll Tide!"

"Damn glad to hear that!" the manager said, and continued, "did I mention the ten percent discount at signing of the contract and another ten percent for being military? Oh, and feel free to grab one of those Bama bumper stickers on the front desk when you leave."

"Why, thank you!" Reggie said with a sigh of relief, and only partially because of the decrease in the rent he now anticipated.

****

And, Montgomery, Alabama is where he had met Alicia and they were now married expecting their first child in about five and a half months, and he had just been promoted to Technical Sergeant and his date to "pin on" the new rank was next month. The pay increase would come in handy too! He was going to use the first few months of the pay increase to take Alicia on the honeymoon they had never had. They were going to the Bahamas!

****

Reggie had met Alicia one day in the local Mall parking lot of all places. He had run in to the food court to make a food run for the guys in the office. That particular month he was a little tight on funds and the old Air Force rule was "you fly and I'll buy." What that meant was he had agreed to make the food run if the other guys bought his lunch. So he came out of the mall food court in a hurry with a large bag of Chinese food and a couple of burgers when he saw her standing there beside the rear passenger side tire of her car.

Alicia was not just the prettiest black girl he had ever seen, she was the prettiest girl of any complexion he had ever seen, period! She was standing there staring at the right rear of her car and looking totally disgusted with her hands on her hips and glaring at the tire as if it had just insulted her.

Reggie saw the flat tire and without hesitation he said, "Excuse me miss, can I help you?"

This penetrated Alicia's disgust and she looked up as though seeing him for the first time. The tall white guy with the big arms and a big bag of food had just spoken to her. Something about help? "I'm sorry," she said "were you talking to me?"

"Yes, ma'am, can I help you?" Reggie repeated.

Alicia switched on a thousand watt smile and said, "You sure can, if you have the time."

"OK then, let me put this bag of food into my car right over there and I will be right back." He turned away then turned back, "Do you have a spare tire?"

"I think so," she said, "but I don't have the thingie to take the screws off."

Reggie was doing all he could not to laugh out loud

at her response. "No problem, I think I have a 'thingie' in the trunk of my car that might work." Then he continued to his car smiling all the way, but since he was facing away from her she could not see the humor he found in this whole situation. Reggie put the food on the back seat of his car and then opened his trunk.

When he walked back over to Alicia he had the lug wrench in one hand and was unbuttoning his uniform shirt with the other hand. He laid the lug wrench on the asphalt and removed his light blue shirt with all the military stuff on it and hung it on the antenna of her car explaining, "I don't want to get my uniform dirty."

****

She just nodded understanding but she didn't say anything. In fact she was glad he couldn't see how much she was enjoying the scene as he opened the trunk of her car. He wrestled the spare tire out of its hiding place, assembled the jack and used it to lift the car in preparation for the actual tire changing. His arms bulged with the strain of a couple of the lug nuts that had rusted in place and the muscles across his shoulders flexed as he removed the flat tire and then seated the spare tire where the flat had been.

This white boy had obviously been in the gym a lot, and she meant a lot, or he had done a lot of manual labor in the past. Or, maybe it was both. In any event, it was worth the delay in her schedule to see this. And, he was so polite, she thought.

In a couple of more minutes he had placed the flat spare tire in the truck of her car along with the pieces of the car jack. Reggie then produced a small bottle of hand cleaner from somewhere and cleaned his hands on a handkerchief he took from his back pocket. Then he pulled his uniform shirt from the car's antenna and quickly put it back on tucking the shirt tail into his dark blue uniform pants as the last step. She could see from the ease with which he did this he had a narrow waist and a very firm belly.

****

Alicia broke out of her little daydream and asked, "How much do I owe you?"

"Ma'am, I am SSgt Reginald Smith and you don't owe me anything at all. Remember, I asked you if I could help you. And you agreed to let me do so. I am paid by the federal government so think of it as an early refund on your taxes." As he said this last he smiled and winked at her.

He likes me, she thought. This white boy is flirting with me. She held out her hand , "Well Staff Sergeant, my name is Alicia and I certainly do appreciate your help."

Reggie took her hand and shook it but did not let it go immediately, "Do you appreciate it enough to let me buy you supper tonight?"

"How about we meet for a cup of coffee and some small talk first. Then we will see if we even like each other enough, OK?"

Reggie let her have her hand back, "Yeah, I guess that was a little fast, huh? Can I get your name?"

"Alicia. My name is Alicia. And, how about we meet at that little coffee shop across the street over there, say about five thirty?"

"Alicia, call me Reggie, and five thirty would be perfect but right now, I better get this food back to my buddies or I will face a hungry group of guys this afternoon. Five thirty, then?"

92

"Five thirty." Alicia said and turned to get into her car. She was pleased to see that he waited for her to leave first, and that he even opened the door for her, and waited for her to pull away before turning back to his own car.

****

Back at the office the rest of the guys started giving him a hard time about taking his own sweet time with the food but when he told them he had helped a lady change her tire they backed off the jibes. That afternoon he left promptly at four o'clock, went to his apartment and showered before putting on a pair of jeans and a clean polo shirt. Reggie was at the coffee shop ten minutes early and waiting for her to show.

Alicia was right on time and beamed at him as he stood to greet her when she walked in. They got into the line for coffee which he paid for and retreated to a table in the corner to nurse the hot beverages. "So, what can you tell me about Alicia?" He asked between sips.

"What do you want to know?" She replied.

"Maybe your last name, phone number and address?" He said.

"My name is Alicia Johnson, and that is all you need to know for now."

They started slowly but began to warm to each other as they got to the end of the cup. Then she asked the inevitable question, "So, Reggie do you root for Auburn or the University of Alabama?"

"Bama!" He blurted almost automatically, and maybe a little proudly.

Alicia shook her head and looked down at the cup in her hands. "See, and I was just starting to like you too. My family all pull for Auburn."

Reggie looked crestfallen so she reached out and placed her hand on top of his. "But, you can always change teams." She was teasing him but she could see he wasn't sure.

"Is there any point in asking you for that dinner date?" He asked a little unsure of himself now.

"Yes," she said simply, "but you need to wear your uniform when you come pick me up."

"Oh, why is that?" He asked smiling again.

"Well, I live at home still and you may have noticed the difference in our skin." She started but he cut her off.

"I have noticed yours is a lot smoother and softer than mine." Reggie smiled. Then he added, "And it looks like you might tan a bit darker than I do." And he smiled again.

She really was starting to like this guy but what she said was, "Well, yeah, there is that but my father doesn't have any of those race hang ups. However, with your Bama leanings you are gonna' need something on your side when you meet him standing there in his Auburn T-shirt."

"And you think the uniform will help?" Reggie asked a bit doubtfully.

"Oh, didn't I tell you? My daddy is a retired Air Force Master Sergeant, and now he is a detective on the local police force." She was clearly enjoying Reggie's discomfort as he processed her words.

"So let me get this straight, I met the prettiest girl I have ever seen today and she has agreed to a date." He started and she nodded, "But I, as a redneck white boy from South Carolina, who is descended from a long line of white sharecropper redneck tobacco farmers; and who favors Bama football, have to get past a black man, who is a retired AF senior Non-Commissioned Officer? And that same black man is now an undercover cop and he hates my football team, is that about right?"

"Yes." She said stretching out the word and smiling wider all the time.

"OK, so is 'Class A' uniform enough or do I need my tuxedo equivalent Mess Dress uniform?" But she could see he was smiling now too."

"Oh, I think Class 'A' will be enough, but I did mention he is a Vietnam era combat veteran right?"

"This just gets better and better!" Reggie said as he took her arm and walked her out to her car. When they got to the car, he surprised her by leaning forward and kissing her lightly on the lips. Her eyes came open wide but she kissed him back and did not shove him away.

"Did I say you could do that?" She asked playfully.

"Uh, no, you did not but I figured this may be my only chance given my imminent meeting with your father." He smiled and just stood there looking into her eyes.

Alicia stretched up on tiptoe and said, "Then I won't ask your permission either." And with that she kissed him back. Then Alicia turned her back on him and said over her shoulder as she got into the car, "Shall we say eight o'clock tomorrow evening, the address is in your right front pants pocket." Then she closed the car door, waved to him through the window and drove away.

****

From there it had been a whirlwind courtship that

lasted six and a half months. They were a force of nature and it was clear to all they were meant for each other.

Now three years later, soon to be Technical Sergeant Reggie Smith and Mrs. Alicia Johnson-Smith were as happy as two people could be.

This was still the Deep South and there were a few holdouts who did not like a mixed marriage. However, in truth this was Montgomery, Alabama and there were more and more who considered the racially mixed marriage to be less of a problem than the Bama/Auburn mixed nature of the marriage. And, it was true that during the Iron Bowl while Reggie and Alicia always started in the same room, they did not always finish In the same room. Otherwise, they got along very well.

For starters the support functions at the Air Base were superb and the U.S. Military had long ago worked out any race issues still hiding below the surface. They even went to Mass at the base chapel on Sunday mornings and then to a brunch at the NCO club. In fact they got more stares during football season when they walked along together and he was wearing his red T-shirt with the white BAMA across the front and back and she wore her blue oversized T-shirt with the WAR EAGLE on both sides.

Bahamas

On this day Reggie came into their house on base holding two plane tickets to Eleuthra, Bahamas which he handed to Alicia as he kissed her.

She kissed him back and then looked down at the thing he had handed her. "What's this?"

"Baby, that is the honeymoon we never had. Now is the time, before you deliver our first child. And the pay raise kicks in next month so we can use a few months of that pay difference to pay for it before the money is committed for the baby!"

Alicia took a long minute to think it over but he could see she was warming to the idea. "I'm in!" Alicia said excitedly, she could see his logic was sound and they were due for a little alone time. They both knew their lives would change drastically once the child was born.

They both loved kids and were looking forward to making this family just a little bit bigger. Besides her father had been ecstatic about the pregnancy and his family, while not exactly ecstatic were also supportive. But, they were after all the only mixed race marriage on either side of the family and they expected different degrees of acceptance from different family members.

****

10. HARRY & JANE: SETTLING IN

The sun came up over the Pink Sand Cottage on the Atlantic side of the ocean in an explosion of bright yellows and reds out across a relatively calm morning seascape. Harry tried to shield the light from his eyes with a pillow but Jane would have none of it.

"Hey," she said, "I found the makings of coffee and managed to get enough together for two cups. Get up now and you can have one of them."

Harry gave a very groggy, "Thank you Janie." As he rolled out of bed, stubbed his toe on one of the suitcases and made his way hobbling to the bathroom.

When he came back out of the little bathroom his face had been washed and his hair had apparently had a passing acquaintance with a comb, and so had at least some semblance of order. Harry took the cup of coffee she was holding out to him and focused on the scene through the open door.   "Wow!" He said, "that is beautiful! I have never seen a sunrise so vivid!"

"I know," Jane said, "This place really is beautiful, huh?"

"Yes, it is. Although I do wish it was a little bigger but it will be OK once we get all this stuff put away." Jane said as if she were trying to convince herself. It was obvious that she had over packed again. That of course was an old discussion that she did not want to get into on this trip at this time.

"Just leave it all where it is, Janie. Throw on some clothes and let's find our way to some food, then we can come back and unpack and put away to our heart's content." Harry said.

"Actually that sounds like a good idea." Jane

replied and went to take a quick shower.

Harry was waiting when she came out of the shower for his turn, "You know, it's a little like our first apartment." And with that he reached over and hugged her naked wet body against his.

Jane pushed away, but did it gently, "I was thinking the same thing but if we start acting like we did back then we won't ever get out of here to get something to eat." Then she kissed him and sidestepped to the sink to finish drying herself off.

"Janie, you may not realize it but you look better now than you did back then and I am starting to remember those old feelings . . ." Harry started but Jane cut him off.

"No you don't mister," Jane held up a small manicured index finger, "First you have to feed me!" It was something young lovers might do and say and they were both smiling and feeling pretty good.

They did manage to get showered and dressed quickly, lock the house and head back up the dirt road to the paved highway. It took them to the town between the cottage and the airport and they found Waters Store which sold food on one side and beer on the other side but they continued just a bit further to a little coffee shop that Jane had spotted on the way in. It was called Da Perk and had a lovely outside sitting area with rustic wooden tables and an assortment of benches and brightly colored chairs on which to sit.

They each ordered a breakfast plate with an egg, toast and some fresh fruit and yogurt and a large cup of black coffee. Then they sat and watched some guy across the street as he was putting his boat in the water of the little bay across the road from the coffee shop. It was like the scene on a postcard - the light blue of the little bay framed by the bright yellow of the painted wall beside the road and the white sail of the little boat and they had no schedule and no hard time to be anywhere.

After they ate they just sat there sipping the remainder of the coffee and enjoying each other's company until finally Jane said, "Harry, what happened to us?"

Harry waited a long couple of minutes staring into his coffee cup and finally said quietly, "I don't know, baby, I don't know."

"We lost the magic, and I want it back." Jane continued.

This time Harry responded immediately, "Me too! I want time for us like it used to be; but," he interjected, "I really think this may be a longer conversation than we have time for right now."

"You're right," she said, "let's put this aside until we get back to the cottage and go get some food and beer to last the next couple of days."

"Sounds good, baby. I want to continue the conversation too but maybe over a glass of wine on the front porch at the cottage, OK?" Harry said as they stood to make their way out to the Jeep.

****

They walked around the crowded aisles of the Waters Store that were barely wide enough for one person pushing a cart. They maneuvered through the shelves that were full to overflowing with everything a store twice it size would carry. Half an hour later they had paid the bill and put the bags into the back of the Jeep. Then they both walked over to the other side of the store to look for beer and wine. They were pleasantly surprised at the selection and found a couple of bottles of a decent Cabernet and asked about the local beer. The owner, Johnson, immediately opened a bottle so they could try it.

Ten minutes later they had four bottles of wine and a case of Kalik beer in the back of the Jeep and we're heading back to the end of the asphalt and down the little dirt road that led to the Pink Sand Cottage. This time, though they weren't lost and they weren't in a hurry and the drive was much, much more pleasant. Jane even tried the radio and was greeted by the strains of **"Uga Chucka, Uga Chucka, I can't stop this feeling, deep inside of me, girl you just don't realize what you do to me!"**

****

It took the rest of the morning to get everything unpacked and put away and by noon Harry was sitting on the little porch on the front of the house with a view of the pink coral sand being caressed and massaged by a calm tide and gentle waves rolling across the beach. Jane came out of the door with two plates and a couple of sandwiches with chips on the side and a couple of fresh bottles of beer.

Harry accepted one of the plates, thanking her, and pulling out the other chair so she could sit beside him. They ate pretty much in silence and watched the tide rolling in over the beach and when they were done with the food Harry picked up the plates and carried them into the kitchen and put them into the sink. Then he came back out and sat beside her on the porch and they just held hands and looked into the sea for a long while before either spoke.

****

Harry said, "This is as good a time as any to start the discussion. There is nobody here except us and we have no deadlines to meet. You want to go first?"

"Yes, I do," Jane said. "First things first, I want to know is do you still love me?"

"What? Baby, I loved you when we got married and I have loved you for all these years and I love you now, and there is nobody else in my life." Harry paused a moment then continued, "Now, my turn, do you still love me?"

"Harry, I have always loved you too, but as time goes on you seem more and more distant and more and more consumed by the factory."

"Fair enough. First it was getting the factory up and started and then getting it to be profitable. And now the expansion has taken a lot of time, I know, but the factory is our main source of income and I have a lot of people depending on me. It's you and the kids and all the expenses that go with the kids but, I also have a lot of people counting on having a job so they can feed their own families."

Jane responded, "I don't want to sound cold or argumentative but it sounds like you are explaining. And, I know you work hard and there is a lot riding on success but why do you pay those assistants so much money if they aren't capable of running things without you?" Jane asked.

"Baby, if they were that good they'd be the boss and I would be the one working for them." Harry came back immediately but it came across like he was bragging and justifying his over control and he knew it. He added, "That may sound egotistical but there are some policy decisions that they just can't make because it is our money and our future they would be gambling with."

She started to speak but he held up a hand to stop her, "No, let me finish, please. Having said that, you need to know it got a little rocky there for a while but everything now is pretty much under control. It's under control to the point I can take more time away from work and spend it with you and the kids, if that is what you want." Harry said.

"Of course that is what I want," Jane replied almost before he had quit speaking, "I could compete with another woman but it is hard to compete with a factory."

"Baby, is that the way you see it? Really? You compete with the factory?" Harry asked somewhat incredulously as if he were just now starting to fully grasp the depth of her discontent.

"Honey," Jane began, "I know this is sensitive but please hear me out. I feel like a single mother with three kids . . ."

"What?" Harry interrupted her.

Jane shot back, "I asked you to hear me out, please. Sometimes I feel like a single mother who has three kids and boyfriend who drops in for a few hours every day or so. And when he does show up there is precious little time for us as a couple and the kids are already asleep so there is almost no time for them."

Then standing up and looking out at the water Jane continued, "I just want you to think about that for a few minutes, don't respond or explain or make excuses, I am just sharing how I feel." Then abruptly shifting the conversation she said, "Let's take a walk down the beach and cool this discussion down before we go any further, right now, shall we?"

****

Harry was in agreement, besides he wanted some time to think and to figure out the best way to change this dynamic. His mind was racing and this was not what he had expected. But in truth he had no idea what he had really expected. This trip had been her idea and he had come along begrudgingly; and he had let her know it. That, he could now see had been a mistake and he didn't want to make things any worse than they already were.

He admitted to himself they had begun to enjoy the last few days. His mind was racing with thoughts and memories and feelings of love for the woman he had married so many years ago. She was also the mother of his children and the single biggest reason he had done all of this in the first place. Yes, he thought he did truly love her but she no longer knew that in her heart and he had to help restore that feeling. Ever the pragmatist, he also knew instinctively that it didn't matter how they had gotten to this point, there would be time later to go over that in his mind and figure it out.

What mattered right now, right this minute, was that she was still talking to him and the conversation was painful but honest and he needed to keep it going. The walk was a good idea. It meant time to think and to be close to her at the same time and it meant changing scenery and right now that might be a very good thing.

"OK," Harry said, "I understand what you're saying and I can respect how you feel, let's take that walk. We can talk some more later today or maybe

104

even tomorrow. Let's take that walk. Right now a stroll down the beach might be perfect."

And it was perfect. The breeze was warm and the sea was rolling out in a gentle tide. The sun warmed them and they held hands and strolled in an unhurried way.

****

11. HARRY & JANE: THE DISCUSSION CONTINUES

The tide was just starting to turn back in when Harry and Jane made it back to the cottage. They had left walking side by side, but the difference now was that Harry had his arm around her shoulders and she had her arm around his waist. This is how they had walked together when they had first started dating, and that was a good sign. Somehow the feel of each other's presence had become more important than finishing the discussion for the rest of their stroll alone on the pink sands, just the two of them.

"Look at that," Harry said from about thirty yards away from the cottage, "Isn't that beautiful? You were right, this place is magical."

Jane agreed that it was a perfect beach scene with the berm covered in the bright green sea lettuce, and the wooden stairs up to the large sunning deck on left side at the top of the wooden stairs. And the short path to the porch on the right at the top of the stairs. More importantly she was feeling warm towards Harry. "Yes, she said, it is magical, but we better get back up those stairs. I can smell the rain in the air and that little black cloud over there is coming this way."

They scrambled up the stairs and just made it under cover of the porch. The wind picked up and the palm trees leaned just a bit but the two of them just stood there holding each other as the first drops blew in on the wind.

"Come inside Janie," Harry said pulling her gently through the door.

They stopped just inside the doorway and just held

each other watching the rain fall as occasional errant drops splashed onto the floor of the porch. Then she turned into him and they kissed in a warm embrace that ended on the bed. They forgot about the rain and focused on the warmth of each other's bodies. The two of them melted together in a tangle of arms and legs on top of the bed in broad daylight with the door to the porch standing open and not caring about anything except each other.

****

The rest of the afternoon they just lay together, listened to soft jazz on the stereo, sipped a couple of glasses of wine and watched the rain falling outside. Eventually they fell asleep in each other's arms. Sometime in the middle of the night Jane got up and closed the door. Then she pulled a blanket over them and snuggled back beside Harry.

****

The next morning she awoke to the smell of coffee and the noise of a man trying to be quiet in the kitchen. Harry heard her starting to stretch and move on the bed and he walked over carrying a cup of coffee and a plate with toast, and butter, and fresh jam.

Jane sat up gathering the covers around herself. They sat and ate together in the morning sun streaming through the window of the door and the windows on both sides of the door.

"What do you feel like doing?" Harry asked as he took the plate back to the kitchen area and refilled the coffee cups. He brought the two mugs back to the side of the bed and offered her one.

Jane took the cup he held out to her and said, "I'd like to go somewhere and see something spectacular today. I saw on the website about some scary looking natural rock formations carved out by the water."

"I'm in!" Harry said, "Sounds good to me."

****

A couple of hours later they were passing through Gregory Town heading in the direction of North Eleuthra and searching for Glass Window Bridge. The bridge was famous for its display of the raw power of nature. She had read about this phenomenon before coming here and it fascinated her.

They found it! They were on the narrowest part of the island and as the fellow in Gregory Town had told them, this was one of the most dangerous places on earth. The fellow had explained how even on a calm day there can be a "rage" which comes out of nowhere. "So, look carefully and then do not waste time getting across the bridge!" he had told them.

A "rage" is what the locals call the huge waves that roll towards the island. There is no barrier reef, so they roll in from somewhere far out in the Atlantic, and without warning. The rage on Halloween Day in 1991 actually dislocated one end of the bridge by eleven feet.

The cliffs tower eighty feet or more above the surface of Atlantic Ocean, and these cliffs force the waves like a sort of rock funnel. As we said before, the waves are forced against the narrow concave cliffs with the power to lift boulders the size of a large piece of furniture.

So even on a clear sunny day these rages can erupt without warning and sweep away any and all unlucky enough to be on the bridge when they occur. There is no discernible season and no discernible cycle. There is just the raw power of nature exerting itself sporadically.

Suddenly, Jane felt the rush of adrenaline as they approached the bridge. The sheer height of the surrounding cliffs left them blind to the scene until actually entering the bridge. The Atlantic Ocean was heaving and rolling on the right and the Bight of Eleuthra was deceptively calm and serene on the left. Jane found herself urging Harry not to spend too much time crossing the bridge. Just as she finished urging him to move on, a wave that must have been fifty feet broke below them under the right side of the bridge.

****

They both breathed easier when they had finished the transit to the other side of the bridge. Harry found a place to pull over and they just sat there a minute sharing a bottle of cola. Then Harry said, "I've been thinking about the discussion yesterday and I have something I need to say."

"Sure," Jane replied, "that's what this time alone is all about." She reached over and touched his leg as if to reassure him.

"Please don't take this the wrong way, but I have been feeling under appreciated and maybe a little like I'm being taken for granted." Jane looked at him a little confused but patted his knee indicating he should continue. "See, baby, from my perspective I have been putting an incredible effort in to making this factory profitable and self-sustaining success since it is our long term security."

Harry looked at her as she soaked in his words, "If I fail, we have nothing. So failure has just not been an option and still is not an option. I have been trying to get to the point you were talking about yesterday, when my assistants can keep things running and we can literally relax and reap the benefits and we are almost there."

She looked serious but nodded for him to continue, so he did, "The kids will be ready for college sooner than we would like, and the mortgage is not yet paid off and we really need a newer car. Then there is the orthodontist, and the sports fees, and the things we want to give the kids, and the list just goes on and on.

Baby, remember when we first started, you used to give me some of the best advice I have ever gotten during the start-up of the business. But every time I try to bring it into the conversation now, you change the subject or shut it down. That makes me feel like you no longer care . . ."

Jane raised a hand to cut him off, "Honey, we have been fools!"

That stopped Harry in his tracks and the look on his face might as well have included a large question mark drawn in the middle of his forehead.

Jane continued quickly, "Don't you see, I have been feeling shut out and in second place to your 'mistress' the factory; and you have been feeling shut out and second place to everything I do on a daily basis. And yet if yesterday and today are any indication, we can still be good together . . ."

This time he cut her off, "Not can be, baby, we are good together!"

"We just have to take the time to do it." Jane said.

"Yep, we just need to take the time to do it." Harry repeated her words with a smile and raised her hand from his knee and kissed it. "Baby, I love you."

"I love you too."

That's when the local constabulary pulled up beside

them and motioned for them to roll down the window, "Everything all right?" The officer asked.

"Yes, officer, everything is very all right. We were just admiring the view, this is really beautiful." Harry said through the open window.

"OK, then." the man in uniform said, "Just don't be here too long, you never know when a rage will come and we have lost tourists around here before."

"Thank you for the warning. We will be going now." Harry waved to the officer as they pulled away slowly onto the road then turned to look over at Jane, "And in this case two tourists have not been lost. If anything but may have just 'found' everything."

This time, she pulled his hand to her lips and kissed his fingers. "Let's go back to the cottage, I think I smell rain again." She said with a big smile on her face.

They drove back in relative silence, at least until Jane remembered there was a cassette in the player so she turned it on and the strains of "Uga-chucka-Uga-chucka, I can't stand this feeling," blared from the speakers and they sang along.

Harry and Jane returned to the cottage arriving about nightfall and spent the remainder of their time there. They barely left the place, except for the long walks every day. They could be seen arm in arm up and down the beach laughing and talking and acting like people half their age.

****

12. ERICA & JOHN: ARRIVAL AND MET BY JAMISON

Erica and John were just finishing their coffee with Jamison as Harry and Jane drove up in the Jeep. Jamison stepped forward with a big smile and asked, "Any issues with the vehicle?"

"None." Harry answered and returned Jamison's smile.

"Good, then, this couple is about to take it over and in fact I believe they are staying in the place you have just left."

At this Jane got interested and entered the conversation, "Hi, I'm Jane and this is my husband, Harry. Are you renting the Pink Sand Cottage?"

Erica answered before John could, "Yes, and I am Erica and this is John." The ladies shook hands and the men also did so. Then there was that awkward reaching over each other as the men greeted each of the ladies and everyone was smiling.

"Have you been before?" Jane asked.

"No, I have not, but John has. This is my first time." Erica said which got a raised eyebrow from Jane.

John jumped into the conversation, "I came here once before to the beach with a group doing some diving as part of an environmental survey. It just seemed too nice a place not to come back to with someone special."

"Well you are going to love it." Jane said as she slid her arm around Harry's waist and he placed his arm over her shoulder.

Erica and John thanked them and tossed their backpacks onto the back seat. When Harry and Jane saw this they both looked at each other and then burst into laughter. Erica and John just looked a little confused. Harry spoke, "Sorry, guys, we are not laughing at you, this is an inside joke between us," as he waved at their luggage lined up on the sidewalk, "my bride might be in the habit of packing a little on the heavy side."

The four of them looked at the two backpacks on the back seat then to the line of suitcases on the walk and back to each other and the four of them started giggling. Somehow it was funny.

Everyone was still smiling as Erica and John drove off.

At Home With Jamison, Sunny and Sweetness

That evening Jamison set the table as his wife, Sunny, and her sister, Sweetness finished up in the kitchen. It was a large rambling house and even Jamison's sister-in-law had her own mini apartment. It was a home from another era and in fact it was the family home Jamison had inherited from his father. The three of them took their meals in the common area most nights.

"You know," Jamison started, "Sunny, you surely embarrassed that young couple this morning with your questioning."

"Well, I know," Sunny answered him, "but it was a slow day and I was bored," Sweetness laughed and Sunny continued, "beside no harm done. We are all adults here and they were smiling too before it was over."

"Well, I'm going to tell the priest what you did

next time I see him," Jamison teased.

"No, don't do that! He will make me go to confession again for teasing strangers about sexual relations. I tell you the man has no sense of humor."

"What is my silence worth to you?" Jamison asked and Sweetness laughed again.

"Maybe an extra serving of those plantains that Sweetness made for desert." Sunny replied.

"I thank, you, Sweetness, for all the hard work you do here while my devious wife is thinking up jokes to play on the tourists."

"She has been that way since we were small girls," Sweetness answered, "Sunny was always thinking up ways to get over on people."

"I did not do any such thing! I was the 'good' one between the two of us. And, mind your manners, after all I am the older sister!" Sunny argued.

"Darling sister, you are a little over a year older and if the truth be known you sometimes claim to be the younger."

Sunny drew up to her full height but before she could start to protest, Jamison cut in, "Yes, I see it all now, we'll have to go to church an hour early on Sunday just so that my wife can go to confession for the other offense we were just discussing and now of course for lying as well by misrepresenting her age."

"Don't threaten me, Mister Smith, there'll be no plantains for you with fresh honey drizzled on them. No sir, not tonight." Sunny teased him in mock stubbornness.

"Don't worry, Jamie, I made them and I'll make sure you get a serving," Sweetness said.

Sunny turned to her and said, "Sweetness, I am

shocked. My own dear sister is conspiring with my husband against me, in my own house. What is the world coming to?"

"Ladies," Jamison cut in, "as delightful as this is and as delightful as you both are, what the world is coming to is supper time. So, shall we join hands and thank God for our food?"

****

The Catholics on Eleuthra were a relatively small congregation and they met on Sunday morning at Saint Paul Catholic Church of the Archdiocese of Nassau. The church is located just off the Queen's Highway with a beautiful view of the Laughing Bird Cay and the Govenor's Harbour Ferry Dock across Haynes Avenue and it is nestled in among the trees.

It was a friendly congregation and sometimes Jamison and Sunny, with Sweetness tagging along, would go for Sunday services and see some of the same tourists who had come through the airport. Art and Samantha for example, had been to worship with them almost every time they had come to the Island. These two older folk from the States were such a wonderful couple and everyone liked them.

Sweetness did not know why Art and Sam had just "walked through her thoughts" but she did reflect that this last time when they had come a few days ago, Mr. Arthur looked a bit worn down. Maybe he had been a little tired but it was clear that Mrs. Samantha was stressed. Women could see these things, she knew, even if the men could not. She had heard a rumor that he was sick. If true that might explain the stress on the lady. She would make a point of saying a prayer for them the next Sunday at Saint Paul's.

After all, that just seemed the proper thing to do. People in Eleuthra were good at that, doing the proper thing at the proper time – not to intrude into people's lives just to offer a little help or compassion when it was needed most. They were generally less bound by traditions and mores of other places and very resourceful about getting things done in a way that everybody benefited. Maybe that was how the island and its people had survived and thrived all these centuries.

****

Sunny was still convinced that somehow Jamison had known in his heart the two girls, she and her sister, would comfort each other just as they had when they were small girls, and he was always such a gentleman. She reflected a minute on the sequence of events that had started so badly with her mother's sudden illness and had ended sadly at first with her death, then everything changed.

Yes, their mother's death was a good example. When that happened she literally had no place to go. But that crisis had worked out well because Jamison and Sunny had unselfishly invited her into their home and everything had worked out for the best well despite the loss of their mother. And they all still enjoyed each other's company and the little jokes and traditions that made it all work so well. The house was a large rambling affair and with three incomes they had no problem with the maintenance of the place. Yes, it was all good and she was still young enough to start her own family if the Good Lord ever sent the right man her way. . . and He had; and she was happy.

13. ERICA & JOHN: TALK & TALK

"This is so beautiful!" Erica said as they made it up the stairs and out onto the deck. "This is everything you said it would be and the pictures you showed me do not do it justice!" With that Erica turned toward John and hugged him.

"So, I take it you are not disappointed?" he said jokingly and hugged her in return. She did not move and if anything leaned against him just a little more. They both felt the warmth rising between them.

"Not at all," she continued after a moment. Then she continued, "And you say there is no one around?"

"Effectively, no. The owner's house back behind us is closed up because they are in the States right now. The place down the beach to the left is up for sale so it is empty. And, the next cottage on the beach was about half a mile ago as we drove here, so yes, we are very much alone here. Why?"

Erica winked at him, "Because I am starting to think that I might have over packed!" And with that she pulled the T-shirt off over her head, quickly wriggled out of her jeans as she kicked off her sandals and stood there completely naked for about half a second. Then she turned and over her shoulder said to John, "I'm going in the water, you coming?"

John followed as quickly as he could after dropping his pants and unbuttoning his shirt and letting it fall. He was not known for being shy, but he was not nearly as uninhibited as Erica was. That was part of what he loved about her, she kept him guessing and was always able to surprise him. She sure made life interesting!

They ran into and out of the water and up onto the beach and finally into each others arms. They held each other and they kissed each other slowly, warmly and deeply. The kiss ended with a slow stroll arm in arm back up the stairs to the front porch of the cottage. They picked up their discarded clothes, went inside and closed the door.

****

John and Erica made love several times during the night and awoke with the sun streaming through the shutters. They were still holding each other. She opened her eyes, looked at him and smiled, "What, no run this morning?"

He yawned and said sleepily, "Actually I was waiting for you to see if you wanted to join me in my morning exercise."

"Liar," she said and hit him with her pillow. "You were hard and fast asleep until about two seconds ago."

"Yeah, I know. And it was glorious!" John smiled at her and started to get out of bed.

"You're not really going to run right now, are you?" she asked.

"No, baby," he said, "maybe later. Right now I thought I would either shower while you make some coffee or I will make some coffee while you shower. Your choice."

Erica flashed a five hundred watt smile as she started to get out of bed herself and said, "Make mine strong and black this morning. I am going to get the first shower."

"Yes ma'am." John said and slapped her playfully on the butt as she brushed past him in the small kitchen to get into the bathroom. He smiled to himself as he heard her singing in the shower.

****

By the time Erica came out with towel dry hair, that gave her a clean scrubbed look, and wearing a long T-shirt, John had set two cups black coffee on the little bar table. Erica pulled up one of the barstools on the side across from John, who had his back to her facing the kitchen counter.

He turned around holding a plate of toasted bread, fresh butter and she saw open jars of jam on the counter behind him. "Does this meet with your approval?" he asked in mock sincerity.

"In deed it does, sir," Erica replied holding the coffee cup in both hands and blowing across the top of the steaming liquid. "But, where did you get all the other stuff?" she asked.

I told you I have used this place before and I got to know the lady and her daughter who clean this place between guests. I had the owners ask her to leave a little breakfast food in the cabinet and voila!" he said with a flourish.

"You are a man of many surprises." Erica flashed that five hundred watt smile again.

"Well, you enjoy and I will take the next step in my plan to keep you smiling."

"Oh, and what's that?" she asked.

"I am going to take a long hot shower and put on some sexy cologne that, according to the advertisement is guaranteed to win your heart." John said and gave her his own warm smile.

"I can hardly wait." She said as he ducked into the little bathroom and closed the door. The coffee tasted good and the fresh bread and sweets were heavenly.

Erica had to admit to herself that John had just moved up a couple of notches in her personal ranking system. He was just so thoughtful and caring.

****

Of course she realized he was also a hardnosed business man and a rising star as a young banker. She assumed that people didn't just rise in banking because they were "nice guys" so he must have a hard side in there somewhere. Or maybe, she almost said aloud, maybe he is just really good at separating the two. Maybe he compartmentalizes the business stuff and keeps it away from the personal stuff.

She wanted some more time to think on that but right now what she wanted was more coffee. And there was the remainder of his coffee just sitting there getting cold. He wouldn't mind; she was sure. She had just touched the cup to her lip when the bathroom door opened with a flourish.

In truth it wasn't a real door but a louvered door to allow air flow in and out of the bathroom. And she realized he could see her through the louvers from the bathroom. And there he was, still damp but clean shaven with his hair pushed back and dripping as he toweled himself in the open doorway. Aside from the towel he was not wearing anything and she liked the view.

"Caught you!" he said. Then in mock accusation he said, "Coffee thief!"

"More like 'coffee borrower'," she said as she took the first sip and smiled at him.

"Absolutely, not! Ma'am this is my business! As a banker I understand these things and I do not see any evidence of a promissory note or a pledge for repayment. No ma'am, you are an unrepentant, coffee thief caught red handed in the act!"

Erica set the cup on the counter and walked as sensuously as she could, the three steps to the open door of the bathroom, and said in a breathy voice, "Why kind sir, what can I ever do to make amends for this innocent transgression?"

Then she reached up on tiptoes and kissed him as she reached behind him with both hands and took the cheeks of his butt in her warm hands.

As nature took its course and his erection pressed against her she smiled through the kiss and said, "Well, would you look at that, it appears we may have a solution to the dilemma." The Erica released his cheeks, placed one hand against his chest to push gently as she took his erection n the other hand and literally steered him backwards across the room to the bed they had so recently vacated.

****

An hour later they were in the Jeep joking and laughing and trying to remember to drive on the wrong side of the road. They were headed back in to town in search of food. John had previous experience at the Waters' Store and he knew that Erica would find it charming – crowded but charming. But first, they were headed to the new place that Jamison had told him about, Da Perk which, according to Jamison was both a coffee shop and a restaurant.

They found it easily with its quaint white frame building and white picket fence around the outdoor sitting area filled with the brightly painted red, yellow and blue tables and benches. From the sitting area they could see the beautiful little bay across the Queen's

Highway and the bright yellow painted low retaining wall across the street. Erica stopped for a minute taking it all in and John asked if everything was all right.

Erica did not respond immediately but she turned into him and hugged him around the waist and then said into his chest, "Yes, everything is very good, thank you for bringing me here. You were right, this place is magical."

John lightened the mood by holding her at arms length, looking down into her eyes and saying, "And I haven't even bought you lunch and a latte yet!" That broke the tension and they both laughed and turned into the door that was the entrance of the place.

They ordered two large sandwiches and two latte coffees and indicated they would be outside at a table. The man behind the bar said to wait just a moment and they could take the lattes with them and he would bring out the sandwiches when they were ready.

John paid and carried the coffees out to the sitting area. Erica pointed towards a empty table right by the fence by the road and they settled in across from each other. They held left hands across the top of the table while sipping the coffee with their free hands.

"Seriously," John asked in his softest voice, "are you OK?"

"Yes. I'll tell you later." Erica responded as the waiter slash barman came out balancing a tray with their food on it. And switching immediately, she gave the waiter one of her best smiles, "This looks fabulous!"

The waiter left the table smiling like he had just been handed a twenty dollar tip.

****

The two young lovers lingered over their lunch and their coffee and eventually made their way after lunch back up the road a block or so to the Waters Store. John stopped as they entered and spoke to the lady behind the register at checkout. "You probably would not remember me, but I was here a couple of years ago."

To his surprise she gushed a warm smile and her face lit up, "Little Johnny, with the divers, right?" the lady said, "you came in every few days for food and beer and entertained my son with your stories about going under water. Welcome back! What is it we can do for you?"

"I am impressed you remember so much! This time I am here with a friend . . ."

"So this must be the lucky girls who is stealing your heart! What is your name dearie?" Mrs. Waters said turning to Erica.

"My name is Erica, and what is yours?"

"Well my parents called me Gladys but everyone else just calls me 'Mom'."

"OK, then, 'Mom' it is. So tell me, was he much trouble when he came here before?"

"Hey, wait a minute . . ." John tried to cut in but Mom spoke over him ignoring his attempt to gain control of the conversation.

"Well all good looking young men are always trouble for the young girls hidden deep inside each of us, but young Johnny was never a problem. Some of the other young men were a little difficult at times but young Johnny here was a perfect angel, but you already know that, girl, or you wouldn't have come all this way with him. Are you serious with him?"

"Look," Erica exclaimed, "he is blushing," as he threw his arms up in surrender.

"Ladies excuse me, I do not have to stand here and be discussed so I shall be shopping."

As he turned away from the two ladies and started deeper into the store Erica continued, "Yes, mom, I think I might be getting serious, I am just not sure he is serious yet. That is part of why I came with him to find out all that I can and see if he might be the one for me."

"Well, Erica, I like you already because you are obviously a straight forward honest girl and frankly Johnny deserves a girls like you. I could tell the last time when he came with the divers that he was different from the others."

"How so?" Erica asked interested.

"He always spoke to me and to my husband next door and greeted everyone. He took time with my boy and told him things the boy did not know. He did not get drunk like the others and then make a lot of racket and disturb everyone." Then she lowered her voice conspiratorially, " And, I did not see him chasing around those euro-trashy girls who always stay in the hotel over there." She nodded over her shoulder indicating some place that Erica obviously did not yet know about.

"Mom, I certainly appreciate your time and your confiding in me," Erica said as she touched the older woman's arm, "but I better make sure he is getting the right stuff to cook. So, excuse me please and I will come back and talk with you again."

"Any time, Erica, anytime." Mrs. Waters said as Erica walked over to join John.

****

"Well that didn't go exactly as I had planned it." John said smiling.

"I thought it went quite well!" Erica said in reply and gave his arm a hug. She liked the exchange on several levels. First she had gained some insight from Mrs. Waters and secondly, it demonstrated that he could be surprised. He tried hard to control all the variables but that was just not always possible.

She had enjoyed his discomfort and his response to losing control of the conversation. For starters he had not gotten upset or angry. And, with that simple response to an unexpected situation, Johnny moved up another notch on her personal ranking scale.

****

The two wandered around the little store collecting one thing and then another they would need for the next few days and loading them into one of the carts that barely fit in the aisle. In this process Erica was the final authority despite John's best efforts to include some extra junk food. When time came to settle the bill they approached the cashier's position by the door but Mrs. Waters had stepped away. Much to his relief, there was no more harassment as John paid the bill.

They loaded the groceries into the back of the jeep then walked over to the other side of the store to pick up some beer and a couple of bottles of wine. Immediately as they walked in through the other door on the front of the building, John and Erica discovered where Mrs. Waters had gone.

****

"My, my, my, Johnny, the wife was right, she is a pretty one! How did you manage to get her to give you the time of day?" Johnson Waters said. This was

Erica's turn to blush.

"Johnson, allow me to introduce the prettiest girl you lot have ever seen and the only girl I ever want to see, this is Erica." John said with the same bravado.

And Erica blushed even brighter red than before but she held out her hand and stepped forward. "Mr. Waters, I am very pleased to meet you." Erica said sounding sincere.

"No, young lady, the pleasure is all mine, I assure you." Johnson responded with a broad smile.

But the smile was cut short, "So, the pleasure is all yours, now, is it, Johnson?" Mrs. Waters was back and she was at the door standing behind the young lovers. But when Erica turned to look at her she winked at the younger woman, and said. "You see the truth of what I was telling you earlier, I have to watch him every minute because he was about to start flirting with you and I would hate to see young Johnny have to get involved to protect your honor." And, she winked again.

Now it was Johnson's turn, "My love, you worry in vain, I have never had eyes for anyone except you." That seemed to satisfy Gladys Waters.

Changing the subject quickly, Johnson asked, "So, Johnny, are you with the divers still? You know, you young people drank a lot of beer back then. It made my business quite profitable that summer." Johnson Waters added.

"No," John answered, "I am a banker now in the Commonwealth of Virginia in a historic old town called Williamsburg. That is where I met this special lady over a cup of coffee. Then I convinced her to come with me to see this beautiful island of yours."

Everyone in the liquor store was smiling. "We just need about a case of beer and a few bottles of wine and then we have to head back to the cottage to finish unpacking."

"Erica," Johnson said turning to the young lady at John's side, "have you ever had Kalik beer?"

"No, Mr. Johnson, I do not believe I have had Kalik."

"Well that is a gap in your education we can cure right now." And before she could respond he produced a glass, popped the top off a bottle and poured half of the bottle into the glass and handed the rest of the bottle to John.

The young couple raised their drinks and John klinked his bottle against her glass and they both took a sip.

"This is quite good." Erica said in obvious sincerity enjoying the cold yellow beverage. "I can see why young Johnny spent so much time coming here for more." And she smiled at John and winked at him. They finished the beer in a very collegial atmosphere that always seemed to be present in the Waters liquor store. Then they said their goodbyes and walked back out to the jeep holding hands.

****

As they started the drive back to the cottage on the beach, John could see that Erica was deep in thought on something. Finally, Erica broke the silence and said, "So, 'little Johnny' impressed them when you were here before; tell me about it, please."

"Not much to tell," John started, "I was in grad school for my MBA and had to take a certain number of classes outside of the department. So being a practical man, I chose one of the marine science courses that included a field trip to the islands. At the time I had no idea what I was getting myself into."

"What do you mean?" Erica asked encouraging him to continue. If the truth be known, she was wanting to know everything she could about him.

"I thought I would just spend the summer carrying an underwater video camera so we could film and collect data for the 'real' science students to use later. It seemed like a good gig for the summer. I thought I could work on my tan, have fun with a bunch of other students and get coursework credit towards graduation – but it was so much more." Then interrupting himself, "Do you know what a cenote is?"

"Yes. I think it is like a sinkhole, right?" Erica looked to him for confirmation.

"Yes, but think of it as much more, think of it as a kind of surface connection to a whole subterranean world. I mean, you are right at a basic level and the most well known cenotes are in the Yucatan. Those are near or at Chichen Itza. But it is not an isolated phenomenon and there are thousands of these things all over the world."

"I didn't know that." Erica said just before they both gasped a little shriek.

After swerving a little to avoid a large white truck barreling down the middle of the Queen's Highway, John continued, "Well that woke me up," and they laughed to ease the tension from the momentary fear. "Where was I? Oh, yeah, see these sinkholes form because the limestone or some other soft rock has been eaten away by the seawater flowing underneath. That process continues and the rock continues to be slowly eroded over time making room for more chunks of rock to collapse. So in that sense, a geological sense if you will, these things are very 'alive' geological features."

John glanced over and saw she had shifted in the passenger seat of the jeep indicating she was at least still listening. He realized he had started to sound more and more like one of his professors had sounded back then. "Then freshwater collects in these sinkholes from rain or runoff or maybe an above ground source of fresh water. But since the fresh water is not as dense as the salt water from the sea . . ."

Erica chimed in with a little laugh like a child learning something new, "I get it, the fresh water floats on top of the sea water, right? And that makes a fresh water pool."

****

"Give the girl in the front row an 'A plus'," John responded with a smile in his voice. Then he continued, "but wait it gets better." It was clear to John that Erica was not only listening but interested.

He took a deep breath and dove in to the topic, so to speak, "Then over time, more connections form and the cenotes, we have found here, may be connected to each other in a Swiss cheese like formations under the ground and under the water. These subterranean networks may be spread over quite large areas."

He glanced over and she nodded that she was still with him. "And since, as you said, the fresh water floats on top and it forms what is called a 'lens' or pool of drinkable fresh water. This fresh water is more or less trapped by the rock formations and that, my beautiful companion happened and is a large part of what happened to make life, as we know it, possible on

Eleuthra."

John continued, "The whole system exists in a remarkable but delicate balance, aided of course by modern de-salinization technology, and good water management. And, that is why on the island we should always shower with a friend." He glanced over to see if she was still listening.

"Sounds good to me," she said, "let's conserve that fresh water as much as we can!" She reached over and squeezed his hand and added, "But, as interesting as that was, you still haven't told me much about John. I want to know everything there is to know about John, and his alter-ego 'little Johnny' that all the people around here seem to know.

****

"Well, Little Johnny met a girl that summer and it did not end well. I liked her and she liked me but she liked some of the other guys in the group even a little bit more that she liked me. Frankly, I did not realize that until it was a little too late. It's a very sad story and I was well over it before I ever even met you. And, out of that affair came John the hardnosed stuffy banker who has a penchant for over thinking, and over planning, and over controlling things."

"I hadn't noticed." Erica said with a touch of irony and John smiled by way of thanking her for that little kindness. Then she continued, "John, you are hardly stuffy like a traditional banker stereotype. In fact you are one of the most un-stuffy people I know." And, with that she gave him that five hundred watt smile again.

They were pulling up to the cottage so he got away without going into more detail with Erica, at least for now. If the truth be known, that was why he had not been here with anyone else since that summer. Erica was the first person since then with whom he had felt like this, and he was starting to feel she might be the last as well. He just wasn't sure where she was in the relationship yet.

****

Back in the cottage they worked in the little kitchen space preparing some fish and chips together and relishing the forced intimacy of the cramped space. They brushed past each other and touched in a hundred different ways as John peeled the potatoes and Erica sautéed the onions and peppers and coked the fillets with just the right amount of everything.

When the smells filled the place and their gastric juices were controlling their thoughts, they started taking the plates and flatware and food outside to the little deck on the front of the cottage. They served the meal on the little table in the corner of the porch outside with a view that was so beautiful it made one never want to leave.

****

Then in an uncharacteristic little ritual that neither expected and that felt so natural they held hands and Erica said a little prayer she had learned in catechism class for her first communion. Then she released his hand and crossed herself in an automatic gesture and saw him do the same thing. "How did I not know you were a Catholic?" she asked.

"Probably the same way I did not know you were," he answered, "we never got around to asking. Of course I am not exactly practicing right now . . ."

"Me either," Erica added immediately and

continued, "but it was a big part of my life once and likely will be again someday."

"Erica, I would also like to be a part of that 'someday' you keep talking about." Then he took a deep breath and continued, "This isn't exactly fair to spring this on you in an idyllic setting with a scrumptious meal awaiting our enjoyment and a view to die for, but this is my perfect day and I hope it never ends."

Erica almost knocked the table over getting up to step over beside him and give John a huge hug and a kiss.

When they broke the hug John continued, "Erica, I am serious. I want this time with you to last forever. I could see us getting engaged in the near future."

"Wow," she tried to joke to lighten the mood as she sat back down, "I have never been engaged to be engaged before."

"Well," John said, "I kind of need time to go with you to every jewelry store back home in Wiliamsburg, Newport News, Hampton, Norfolk and Virginia Beach looking for the perfect ring. Then, I need time to set up the perfect romantic evening with supper at the Trellis or the Blue Talon or the Fat Canary or perhaps even the Elements Restaurant out at Kingsmill on the James with a view of the water in the background. . ."

****

"Stop." Erica said softly, "I see a great meal right here and I see the man I am starting to love. And there is a whole ocean of water behind him; what a view! And I am starting to feel very, very warm inside, now let's just eat and enjoy the time and the company."

They ate and smiled at each other and each one felt

their own pulse just a little elevated and the sun felt warmer, and the food tasted better, and the world was in order. And, there was definitely a smell of rain in the air.

****

John made coffee after the meal and they just sat there letting the food settle as the sun warmed them. In the distance a single boat sailed past. From the outline it looked to be a large cruise ship of some sort and a cloud passed over Erica's face.

John caught the small change in her face and the shift in mood, "What's wrong he asked?"

"That ship out there. I just had a passing thought of my previous trip to Bahamas, that's all."

"Tell me." He said softly.

"That was a long time ago," she demurred.

"If it's a part of you then I want to know." He insisted gently. "After all, you already know most of my secrets, I mean about 'little Johnny' and all."

It had the intended effect. She laughed. "O.K. here's the deal, I will tell you mine but I want to hear all about the girl who broke your heart, because I don't ever want to make the same mistakes she made."

"Honestly, that's the same reason I want to know about your other experience so I don't make the same mistakes and risk loosing the one girl I have been looking for and seeking for so long."

****

Erica's heart fluttered as she took a deep breath and began. "I came on a cruise with a guy named Brad who was, at least at the time, very important to me. The trip came out of Miami and took us to Nassau with several stops along the way."

"Well," John interrupted her, "I did suspect you might have had some experience before I came along." Then he smiled.

"Oh, yes," Erica responded, "did I mention the cruise was a topless, clothing optional type of cruise?"

"Uh, no, I don't think you had gotten to that part yet, but please continue. My mind is already racing with images of you in your birthday suit."

"Well, without going into all the lurid details, then let me say that it all started relatively innocently, except that everyone was either topless or naked. Well, at least aboard ship, they were. When we stopped at the ports of call of course people put on clothes to go into the towns. But while I was focused on Brad, he was apparently more focused on my replacement."

"Ouch!" John said with real sympathy in his voice.

"Yeah," she said wiping a tear with the back of her hand. "I get so damn mad even today because I wasted so much time and effort on that loser. You know what he told me?" she asked, obviously still hurting from the experience.

****

"No, baby, what did he say to you?" John said to Erica holding up a finger, "but before you tell me, are you sure you want to open this wound?"

"Yeah, John, I want to get this out so let me start at the beginning O.K.?" He nodded and she continued, "Brad was perfect. He had perfect hair, perfect manners, a perfect smile, and a perfect car. He looked good and he sounded good and he knew it. But before long, I began to realize he was just a little too focused on himself to the exclusion of anyone and everyone else, including me."

134

"That was his mistake and his loss." John said simply.

"I worked hard to make that relationship work and when he dumped me he was so shallow and so disingenuous it really infuriated me and it hurt." John reached over and touched her leg as if to reassure. After a minute she continued, "He had the audacity to tell me, 'Oh, it's not you, it's me,' what a crock that was."

Then getting her second wind she continued, "I mean what the heck is that even supposed to mean? Of course it was me! Believe me he loved himself way too much to blame anything on himself! So, that was just a line. He was feeding me a line!

And, that tells me he was trying to 'play' me like some kind of a fool. We were ending so he obviously had very little feelings for me and he wouldn't even give me the courtesy; no, make that he wouldn't even give me the respect, to tell me the truth. He was feeding me a line!"

"At that moment in time it all became clear." She continued, "I mean, I have always been physical as far as taking care of myself and I worked hard to look as trim as I do. I thought he liked that about me."

"I know I like that part a lot." John interjected with a smile to ease the tension.

"Thank you." She said sincerely, "But he liked it like he enjoyed his fancy watch or his new car. I was just an accessory for the cruise. You know, like window dressing. I was the right look to be seen with naked on a naked cruise. I was just part of his 'perfect' wardrobe!"

"John, that was two years ago and I don't ever

want to go through that again." Then leaning forward very earnestly, " Promise me!" Erica demanded.

****

"Erica, I don't have a problem with truth and I certainly don't have a problem with my ego. I recognize that you are a truly beautiful person, inside and out, and that you have options and I am just thankful that I am the option you have chosen to be with at this moment in time."

Out of the corner of his eye John saw her smile and cry simultaneously and quietly wipe another tear with the back of her hand. Then she abruptly changed her demeanor and said, "OK, now mister, it's your turn. So, tell me about your heartbreak."

****

"Well, I have never been on a clothing optional cruise and about the raciest thing I have ever done was that skinny dip we took the first day here. And, I found that pretty exciting." John took a deep breath and then started quietly and slowly, "I was always pretty naive, I guess, and I fell hard for a girl in some of my classes during my MBA studies. That's how I new about the other courses and I signed up for the one with the divers because she had signed up for it. Kind of obvious, huh?"

"And you came here?" Erica asked.

"Well, actually we stayed in the town but I saw this place as I was out exploring and I asked to look around and the people staying here said yes."

"Really?" Erica asked, "They just let a stranger barge in?"

"No, it wasn't like that. I made myself known and made sure I wasn't going to surprise anybody." She nodded and he continued, "I approached slowly and looked around carefully. Then I came up on the porch and announced myself.

"Then, well, I knocked on the door and I asked politely if I could introduce myself and talk a moment. Well, the guy who must have been close to seventy, and man was he fit, said O.K. and he came out onto the porch. He looked like some old General or something. Like I said he must have been seventy but he looked like he could have kicked my butt. And his wife came out a few minutes later and she didn't seem to mind either."

John could tell that Erica was interested so he continued, "She was younger, or at least not as old as he was, but man did she look 'put together,' you know what I mean?" Erica just nodded again, and he continued, "She also looked very physically fit and very classy. Any how Arthur, that was his name but she called him Art and he called her Sam for Samantha. As I recall, they not only showed me around, they served me a beer and we chatted for a while."

"This was a couple of years ago and they told me they came here every year or so just to get away from it all." John paused to take a drink, "So, anyhow, I decided right then and there that I wanted what they had."

John continued, "My problem is I had not found the right girl yet. I know that now because while I was being open and honest and naive, she was busy auditioning guys to replace me but without the good grace to cut me loose. When I found out what was going on it crushed me."

"I went to town that evening and drank myself into

oblivion and then I packed up and left the island later that week. So, as you say, that is the story without all the lurid details. Erica, baby, all I ask is that you be straight with me, and it sounds like you might want the same thing from me."

****

They sat there a moment longer enjoying the view then she spoke, "Can we go inside and hug a while?"

"I would like that a lot!" John said and they stood and went inside.

****

The next morning John told her over breakfast, "I have a plan for the day, if you are game."

"OK, I'm up for almost anything. So, what is your plan?" Erica asked.

"Let's go diving. If you're game, just pack a couple of things and we will drive to the beach nearest to The Devil's Backbone. We can dive some of the wrecks off the coast. It's near Preacher's Cave and that is another place you should see.

I am pretty sure the guys who took care of the dive team when I was here before will set us up with equipment and tanks and air. After that you will really understand the cenotes and how the whole hydro-tidal-thingie fits together here and why it so important in the grand scheme of things to how this place works.

"I'm in!" Erica said smiling enthusiastically.

****

They made the drive that same morning after breakfast. They just threw a change of clothes into John's backpack and took a couple of sandwiches along for the trip. It was pleasant and they fell into a comfortable silence, like lovers who have been together a long, long time. He would occasionally reach over and touch her thigh and she would reciprocate with a caress of his hand. It was a bright sunny day and they were both feeling very warm towards each other.

Finally Erica broke the silence, "John," she said quietly, "thank you for opening up last night and for letting me open up on you."

"Baby, you don't have to say anything . . ." John started but she cut him off.

"Yes, I do," she said quietly, "I needed that."

"Actually, I did too," John confessed, "I have never drug that out and somehow it wasn't so bitter after I got it out. I can talk to you like I have never been able to talk to anyone before."

Erica squeezed his hand and said, "I know, I know." Then she added, "So tell me again about being engaged to be engaged."

****

John braked the vehicle quickly and pulled to the side of the road then turned towards her in his seat. "I was absolutely serious, and I now I don't have a ring or anything I am supposed to have . . ."

"Oh, my God!" Erica interjected.

John squeezed her hand, willing her to say yes, ". . . but, Erica, would you be my wife? I want to be with you more than anyone else I have ever known. I want to be with you for the rest of our lives."

Erica turned in her seat, released the seat belt and almost climbed over the gear shift lunging to throw her arms around his neck. Then she just held him and a moment and when she released him he saw a tear on her cheek.

"So, is that a 'yes' or a 'no'?" John asked as he

wiped the tear off her cheek.

"Dummy!" Erica said with a laugh. "That is a 'yes,' definitely a yes, and this is a tear of happiness," she added kissing the back of his hand where the tear had been.

"Baby, we'll go shopping for a ring as soon as we get back home . . ."

Erica put a finger across his lips to quiet his words then she pulled the finger away and kissed him again and settled herself again into the passenger seat.

"We can get the ring when we get back, but today you promised me a diving trip."

"Whatever you say," John said, "whatever you say."

****

Erica turned on the Jeep's stereo system and did a quick scan of all three of the radio stations she could pick up. Then she hit the tape button and the familiar sounds of **"Uga-chucka-uga-chucka, I can't stand the feeling . . ."** came out of the speakers and the two of them sang along with the music.

They got to the area in the late morning and John managed to find one of the guys he knew from the days of the diving survey and they were shortly set-up with gear and a fresh charge of air in the tanks. Erica had snorkeled before but this was her first time with a scuba tank so a quick orientation briefing was in order.

Then John took her out into he water behind the shop and she fitted the device into her mouth as instructed. The most surprising thing was that the air was not automatically "there" and she had to suck in and then force the breath back out.

Like most first time drivers she then breathed

140

immediately again just to make sure it worked and then again. And, pretty soon the "twenty minute tank" was empty. She signaled to John and they surfaced and waded the few yards to the shallow water. "Wow," she said still gasping a little, "is that all the time you get from one of these things?"

"No." John and the shop owner said simultaneously. John continued, "That's why we are doing this here. Now, can we tell you what you did wrong?"

"Yes, Mr. smarty pants, tell me what I did wrong." She had caught her breath and was smiling again.

"Well, you need to trust your system. The air will be there when you need it. You just proved that to yourself, it worked every time you took a breath didn't it?"

"Yes," she said beginning to understand, "I consumed the tank of air but I did not 'use' it!" as the realization sank in.

"This girl is smart, Johnny," his friend, who was also the shop's owner, took over. "See, Erica, the trick is to only pull more air into your lungs when you need it. The truth is that your body only needs new air when you use up the old air so try to slow down your breathing and practice breath control."

"I won't be with you but Johnny will be and he is experienced, very experienced. You will be fine, but next time don't forget about the reserve we showed you on the tank, OK? When you start to run out there is still enough of a reserve to get you safely to the surface."

"One more thing," John said, "we will be starting with snorkel gear on the surface and only using the tank when we want to go down for a closer look at one of the wrecks."

"You going out to Devil's Backbone?" The shop owner asked. Then he added, "It's a "little rough to make it out there from the shore, ain't it?"

"No problem, Sonny," John said to the owner, "I got a boat lined up. One of the guys we used before. He will take us out and stay around on the surface if we have any problems."

"O.K. Little Johnny, you always were careful and that is good, my man, very good." Then back to Erica, "You definitely smart girl to go out with Little Johnny, he always has back-up plans!"

Erica flashed Sonny her five hundred watt smile. Then they loaded the equipment into the back of the Jeep. "I will have it back to you tonight, OK Sonny?"

"O.K. man, you two have fun today. But, if the shop is closed just leave the equipment out back. You know the place, like you used to do."

"No problem, my friend." John said.

****

"So," Erica said, "This guy also called you Little Johnny, why? And he was not the first time that I have heard that. What is that all about?"

"You mean, how did I get that nickname?"

"Yes, exactly. I want to know everything there is to know about you!" She said and reached over and touched his hand.

"When I came down here before, with the grad school diving project, there were a bunch of big hulking sports guys and very fit girls. I am not normally found in that group, you may have noticed." And he smiled at her. She smiled back.

"I mean," he continued, "I am fit and I take fitness

142

seriously but I am more of a runner with a little weight training, not the other way around. So, one of the guys was always giving me a hard time about trying to 'play with the big boys' and stuff like that."

"Is that it?" Erica asked.

"Oh, no, not even close. That was just the start. One day he was being a real jerk with one of the girls and I said something to him. I guess it embarrassed him because he took off on a rant about how I should grow up and learn how life works. Then he said something about being in a little kid's world and I should go away 'Little Johnny' and quit bothering the real men. Then he tried to push me. I mean he reached out to shove me in the chest and that's when I snapped."

"What did you do?" Erica asked obviously intrigued.

"Well we were in the middle of the dance floor at that little pub downtown and he had been drinking. So, as he reached out to shove me in the chest, I just stepped to one side and grabbed his wrist and pulled. As I pulled him forward, I was adding my force to his own momentum in the same direction."

John shrugged and continued, "I just placed my right foot just in front of his and he tripped over it. It all worked just like they taught us in that dojo I used to work out in. He went down hard. I mean, he hit the floor like a sack of potatoes and wallowed around getting back to his feet but he had busted his nose and was bleeding from both nostrils."

"Wow, I didn't know you were such a badass!" Erica said clearly impressed.

"Wait, it gets worse," John continued, "That girl he

was harassing walked over to him while he was sitting there trying to stop his nosebleed and threw her drink in his face and said, 'Little Johnny, indeed. Looks to me like the only real man in here!' Then she slapped his face and walked away. He was gone the next day."

John continued the story. "Most of the dive guys, like Sonny who supplied us with gear, were in there that day and they all saw it. The story got around town quickly and the nickname stuck. But I don't mind because they all use it as a sign of affection."

Erica just smiled at him.

"What?" John asked her.

"I came on this trip so I could learn more about you." Erica continued, "And, everything I learn, I like a lot."

"What, that I sometimes have engaged in bar fights?" John said.

"No, that you have what my father would have called 'the courage of your convictions'," she said smiling, "and you are not afraid to take action. And, you plan ahead."

"Except, when it comes to asking a girl to marry me and then not having a ring ready." He said.

"Baby, we have time for everything," she said, "everything!"

John parked the car and found Nathan who had his boat ready to go. They were on the water in a matter of minutes and headed to the dive area.

****

14. REGGIE & ALICIA: ON THE WAY

Reggie had already told his supervisor about the plans he and Alicia had made and she had forwarded the leave request to her boss. In this case the leave time had to be processed and approved all the way to the Commander since Reggie and Alicia were actually leaving the country. But, all of that didn't stop his co-workers from giving him a rash of good natured kidding. And the icing on the cake came on his last day in the shop before they left.

The shop foreman put the word out that she was calling a team meeting. So everyone showed up at about 3:00 in the afternoon for her remarks. Senior Master Sergeant Brenda Sanders walked in and the group settled down immediately. Brenda was a career NCO and ran an extremely efficient operation. She was a no-nonsense black woman with an intense look about her and a gaze that could make any of the guys uncomfortable. One of Reggie's buddies had quipped it was kind of like working for your mother, if your mother was a very fit, tough as nails product of inner city Detroit, with a bad attitude.

"Listen up," the imposing middle aged woman said in a strong clear voice, "there is only one reason we are here and I think you all know why that is?"

Reggie was confused, because if this was an ass chewing he had no clue. Things had been going pretty well and they were ahead of production in the back shop and with the office paperwork. Then he noticed a couple of the guys starting to smile. Somebody rolled a chair up behind him and they pushed him into it. Somebody else ran a strand of duct tape around his arms and chest and at that point resistance was futile.

After a minute of this abuse, he was rolled in front of his supervisor. That is when he noticed that "Senior," as she was called was carrying a bag. With great ceremony and mock seriousness SMSgt Sanders produced a straw hat which she gave to one of his work buddies.

His buddy took the hat like he was carrying a flag and marched over to Reggie's side where he came to attention with the hat held in front of him. At that moment and on cue the Senior said, "Sergeant Reginald Smith, I present you with the proper head gear for a man of leisure vacationing in the islands." With that his buddy planted the straw hat on Reggie's head and put a big rubber band around it to hold the thing in place.

That's when Reggie noticed Alicia walking in from a side door. So, she was in on this too, huh. But Senior Master Sergeant Sanders was talking again, " . . . and, with the one possible lapse in judgment when Alicia said yes to you, I have complete confidence that if you follow her direction she will return you in good working condition when this trip to paradise is over. But, in the meantime, just in case they don't have enough on Eleuthra, here are some of those little umbrellas for the 'island drinks' you will be enjoying."

Then Sanders pulled a pack of little cocktail umbrellas out of the bag and handed them out to his friends who stuck them into his button holes, shirt pockets, behind his ear and basically everywhere they could fit one to make him look ridiculous. "And we wouldn't want you to burn your lilywhite skin down in the islands so we brought you a little sun protection for your nose." With that she stuck a clown nose onto the helpless victim.

Turning to Alicia she said, "Madame I present your traveling partner, perhaps you would pose for a picture?" Alicia immediately bent over and put her pretty face beside his. She smiled her thousand watt smile while Reggie squirmed and resisted the duct tape pinning his arms to the chair.

"Reggie," Sanders said, "these pictures will be available on the unit website and the bulletin board in the main hall of the administrative building before you can even get to your car, so relax."

Reggie just groaned and smiled and laughed with the others as someone finally cut him lose. As he stood his boss spoke again, "Seriously, we all hope you two have a great trip and come back safe and sound. We are going to miss you." Turning to the unit, "In the break room you will find beverages of your choice and I suggest that we are done for the day!"

The noise level went up markedly as they all moved towards the break room. Reggie put his arm around Alicia and kissed her cheek. "Thanks for coming, baby, this was a perfect send off." Alicia just squeezed his hand and kept smiling.

****

The drive home was quiet, in that quiet "I love you way" that young lovers seem to able to fall into effortlessly and that the rest of the world has to work at to attain. Maybe that's because they don't have all the "life experience" to get in the way and provide background noise. They just live in the moment and in each other's hearts.

And that night, with the packing for the trip already

done, they fell into each other's arms making love. They made love with their looks at each other and their words to each other and in all the little ways that really count. They didn't just have sex, although there was plenty of that too, they found a thousand ways to express their love and their feelings and everything seemed to be right with the world when they finally fell into a deep and restful sleep in each other's arms.

****

15. JOHN & ERICA: DEVIL'S BACKBONE

The boat trip to the dive location went without a hitch. Although for Erica's taste, on first glance, the boat was a little too small and a little too primitive but this was after all The Bahamas, and this was not some tourist excursion off Nassau. And, she became more comfortable when it was obvious that the boat's owner and John did in fact know each other and that they moved together like a team performing familiar tasks. The gear was aboard quickly and they were off for the dive.

They set up quickly and deployed a flotation buoy that would trail their diving and alert other boats that they were in the area. On first entry under water she saw the most beautiful underwater scenes. The variety of fish and turtles and the colors of the coral took her breath away.

They were afloat off a sort of reef that had been formed by nature off the north end of the island. It formed jagged edge reef in shallow water. She could also see, even as a novice that the location and the depth made it ideal for snorkeling or for diving.

She could also see what John had been talking about the night before. Those same natural features have made it a serious hazard to boats over the centuries. John had explained that the reef had ripped the bottoms out of more boats than any other reef in the Bahamas.

And he had told her with a wink, "So when you get tired of looking at the fish and turtles there are plenty of wrecks to explore down there."

And there they were, once she shifted her focus she

could see the undersea graveyard. It was clear that this underwater home to marine life and destroyed ships ran from about five feet deep to more than thirty feet deep. The view was awesome as she floated there suspended near the surface.

As they had planned the first dive was just to get acclimated to the water and the temperature. After five minutes or so paddling around using the snorkel gear she climbed onto the dive platform John and the other guy had hung over the side of the boat.

****

John gave her a hand up onto the platform that gave them a shelf on which to sit with the water about wast level. It gave them a place to talk before the dive and on breaks without coming all the way out of the water.

John leaned in to be heard over the dull rumble of wind and the waves, and to smell Erica's hair. She leaned in to hear clearly what he was saying and to be closer to him every way that she could. "The view underwater looks like your favorite seafood restaurant except they are all alive and thriving," John said, "you are going to see snapper, grunts, parrotfish, angelfish and stingrays."

With the possible exception of the stingray, which she was pretty sure she could identify, Erica had no idea what any of these fish looked like. Her closest encounter up until now with some of these fish was under a honey acacia sauce on a rice pilaf, but she smiled at him anyway and nodded.

John took the smile as encouragement and continued, "There is more to see down there than we can see in one day so we will be focusing on one area but it has a couple of notable wrecks in about the same place. We will be looking for the Cienfuegos which was a steam powered American ship about the length of a football field. This thing is huge!" he said warming to his topic. "It was a passenger ship but it ran aground during the first week of February in 1895 and all those steel compartments just lay there like a twisted underwater junkyard. And it makes a really good dive."

"I am really looking forward to this!" Erica said with a genuine smile.

"Wait, it gets better." John said placing a hand on her thigh, "I picked this location because in February 1969 another ship went down in the exact same spot!"

"Was it a passenger ship too?" Erica asked just to keep the closeness of the conversation going.

"No," John replied, clearly enjoying his role as the expert, "the Vanaheim was a costal freighter but it was about ninety feet long and you can see the steel rudder laying maybe five feet off the bow of the Cienfuegos."

John continued, "We don't have time to see it today but there is even a train down there too."

That got a brief reaction from Erica and a momentary look of incredulity, "You, you are kidding, right?"

"No, baby, I am not kidding." John said.

"Back in the mid 1800's a huge barge was carrying a steam locomotive and several train cars and the barge struck a reef during a violent storm. The whole thing went down, barge, engine, cars, everything. Even the coal they had on the barge for the engine is down there. It's in maybe fifteen to twenty feet of water. But like I said we don't have time today to get it all in."

"How many in all?" Erica asked.

"I have no idea, but I have seen the William, sunk in the mid 1600's, the Farmer which sank in the mid 1800's hauling a load of timber from the U.S., and the USS Boston warship which went down in 1846. On that one you can see the old cannon and everything. Oh, and the Carnavon which went down in 1916, that one is pretty and makes for some great photos."

"There are plenty more but those are the ones I have seen."

****

"You know," Erica hugged his arm and put her lips to his ear, "when I told some of my girlfriends I was dating a banker, they said it would last one date because bankers are boring. Boy, were they wrong!" Then she pulled him towards her and kissed his cheek.

John actually blushed, much to Erica's delight. The boat's owner was smiling clearly enjoying this whole little scene. They sat there another minute being close and feeling the wind and the sun on their skin. Then John gave his final instructions, "Any time you feel uncomfortable or uneasy, this platform will be here waiting and we can talk."

****

John and the boat's captain and made a final check of her gear and then he checked John's gear making some minor adjustments. As they leaned forward over the edge of the platform, and off the little platform on the back of the boat, they were immersed in water again.

Erica knew immediately this was different. The quick lesson from John and the instructor had been good but it did not prepare her for the sheer physical experience of being cut off all at once from her normal sensory world.

She felt warm and cold at the same time and there were no sounds except her own breathing and some distant rumbles that had to be the waves and maybe distant boat motors.

She did remember to control her breathing and she began to feel more comfortable. Then she saw John hold up a thumb asking if she was O.K.? She replied with a thumbs up of her own.

John nodded in an exaggerated fashion then used the same thumb to point up to the surface. It was her turn to nod in an exaggerated fashion. Then she gave a little kick of her fins and they broke the surface together.

John pushed his dive mask up on his forehead and said, "Save your air. We can snorkel until we find something interesting then grab the regulator and dive down to take a look."

"Sounds good." Erica said nodding her head in agreement.

They adjusted their dive masks and put the snorkel tubes into their mouths and she swam beside him around the area just taking it all in. Finally he found what he had been looking for and gave the signal. She changed out the snorkel for the regulator mouthpiece and they started down slowly.

Erica knew he was going slowly so that she would have time to adjust. The pressure grew and she became more buoyant, and she understood why the weights around her waist were there. She felt the pressure in her ears more than anyplace else and that took a little getting used to but in a couple of minutes she was feeling comfortable again.

It occurred to her that he had chosen this spot for exactly this reason. True, there was a lot to see but there were things to see at five feet and ten feet and twenty feet and she could become more comfortable as they went. Yep, John always seemed to have a 'plan'. And, frankly she liked that about him.

****

For his part, John was enjoying this immensely. He was like a kid in a candy shop sharing something he really liked with someone he really liked. This was a lot more fun than the last time he had been here, and there was a little twinge of pain with the memory of his 'ex' but that passed as soon as he looked over at Erica obviously smiling around her mouthpiece and wide eyed like a kid on Christmas morning.

****

They had a thoroughly enjoyable day, but it was getting late by the time they finished and they found a little out of the way place and got a room for the night.

****

16. JOHN & ERICA: BACK TO THE COTTAGE

The next morning after breakfast they settled the bill and started back to the cottage. The drive back to Governor's Harbor and the Pink Sand Cottage was perhaps the most pleasant drive that Erica had ever experienced. She was able to share her feelings about the dive experience and the things they had done together and the experiences they now shared. She had never felt this way about anyone.

Oh, sure she had been in love before but this was so much more than that, and she knew it. At this moment in time she could think of nothing she would rather be doing and no place she would rather be than here with this man. She loved the way he looked at her and the pains he took, in order to plan for every foreseeable eventuality. John always seemed to have a "plan B" and to have all the answers to her questions. She liked that too.

At a very basic level it satisfied her security need and she was able to be freer than she had ever felt before. She was confident sharing her innermost thoughts and feelings with him. That was something new! Formerly she only shared such thoughts with a few intimate women friends whom she had known for a very long time. That realization gave her pause and Erica thought about that a moment.

It wasn't like John was replacing them in her life. It was more like he was giving her another outlet for her need for emotional intimacy, and she liked it. She liked it a lot. He always seemed to be there to listen and to give advice when she asked for it but he never intruded into her decision process unless she invited him in. She liked that too.

So they talked and chatted about everything and about nothing in particular. They joked with each other and then shifted into serious topics and back out again to light topics and making each other laugh. She found she really liked his laugh because it came from somewhere down deep and it just sounded "real." And, it was just so damn easy to talk to him. Sometimes it amazed her.

****

When they got tired, they stopped for coffee at a café in a small settlement they passed through. That was something else she liked. John never seemed to grab a coffee "to go," he always had time to find a little café and sit and enjoy the experience. She had asked him about that one time and he had explained the Spanish speaking world's concept of a "sobremesa." Literally, it was a compound word comprised of two words that translated as "over the table" but what it meant is that time during and immediately after a meal, or a coffee, when one can relax and chat.

So they had their little sobremesa and then they drove on until they passed a place that looked like a good risk for seafood and stopped for a leisurely lunch. Of course that was not much of a risk because there is no "bad" fish anywhere in Eleuthera. And eventually they made it back to the cottage.

John carried their one bag up from the jeep and held the door for her to enter first. Erica started in then stopped half way through the door. John was trapped with the bag in one hand and the door in the other. Erica faced him, pressed her body against his, slid her

156

arms up around his neck and kissed him.

"Thank you," she said and when she broke the embrace, "I will never forget yesterday and today." Then she pushed off him and into the little kitchen area.

****

That afternoon and into the evening they sat on the little front porch drinking beer and holding hands and watched the sun and the daylight begin to disappear into a canopy of stars and moonlight. Erica finally stood, took his hand and said, "Come with me. I want to hold you until I fall asleep."

"That sounds like a wonderful idea." John said in reply and followed her into the cottage.

****

They slept throughout the night and John awoke first. The sun was sneaking in through the slats in the shutters giving just enough light for John to make a cup of coffee for the two of then. He made a small pot, poured one cup for himself then moved quietly across the room and out onto the little porch on the front of the cottage. Erica stretched on the bed as he left the room and rolled to her other side taking over the space he had so recently vacated on the bed. He knew she needed a few more minutes before there would be visible signs of life.

Sitting at the little table in the corner of the porch on the side away from the stairs and protected by the house and the palm trees on that side of the house, he began to feel more of the warmth of the sun and less of the morning chill off the water. The coffee cup was warm cupped in his hands as he held the ceramic mug and the strong black brew was still hot to his tongue as he sipped it in silence. It was going to be a perfect day, he could tell.

Of course yesterday had also been a perfect day and it would take some effort to top that one! Still by definition it had to be a good day because they were heading home tomorrow. Their time was up and it was time to put their few clothes back into the back packs and check their paperwork one more time. The only coordination, minimal as it was, was to turn in the car and board the flight back to Fort Lauderdale.

Still he wasn't quite ready to go. He knew they had had a break through in the relationship, he could feel it! He could also feel that they needed a couple of more days to get even closer to each other. This had been a very, very good idea and he was just weighing the options and wondering if she could stay a day or two more than planned in Fort Lauderdale.

John felt good about all of it. He felt comfortable with the relationship and he was doing everything he could not to press too far, too fast but this is what he wanted the rest of his life and he knew that love like this only came along once in a while and maybe only once in a lifetime. Then like blinding flash of the obvious it came to him. He made a decision right then and there, but he held his peace and said nothing right then.

****

Erica and John spent the rest of the day holding each other, just touching and being together. The warmth and the electricity between them was a real and tangible thing. They both felt it and they never wanted to quit.

And just as suddenly the focus shifted from going away from Eleuthra and became the process of going to

158

something else back home in the states. Finally John said, "Erica, can you take some more time off? I'm thinking we spend a couple of extra days in Fort Lauderdale where we won't have the distractions of the daily grind and we can make some real plans."

"I believe I can swing that." Erica said, "just let me make a couple of phone calls as soon as we land."

"No problem. I can use the same time to make some calls of my own and to clear with the hotel, or find another one." John said, "And we can work the airline reservations before we even leave the airport."

****

17. REGGIE & ALICIA: ARRIVAL

Erica was the one up early this morning and it was John who lay in bed a little longer this time. He woke with the noise of her opening the door to the outside as she came in from the little porch on the front of the cottage.

I am a truly blessed, John thought, as he opened his eyes all the way and began to sit up in the bed. Erica was coming back in from a morning coffee on the porch in the pre-dawn glow on the horizon. She stood there a minute highlighted by the glow behind her and John could see that she had her jeans jacket draped loosely over his shoulders but not buttoned. It hung open around her arms as she held the coffee cup in those delicate hands he loved to feel on his skin.

As his gaze continued down from the rise of her slightly tanned breasts to her flat stomach he stopped at her midsection where she had tied a scarf around her waist. The scarf was yellow and peach and orange with a touch of red in the bright swirl of colors that covered her lower body and yet hid nothing. It was almost translucent in the morning light starting to reflect off the water behind her.

"I like that scarf." He said smiling.

"See, I told you, it was a good buy." Erica smiled back at him and came in the rest of the way. She took another step, shrugged her shoulders and the jacket fell away. Then another step as she set the cup down. With yet another step she stepped out of her flip-flops and reached to tug at the knot on her hip.

"Let me." John said simply and she dropped her arms and waited as he fumbled with the loose knot at her hip. "This really is a nice scarf." He said holding it out to one side for an unobstructed view of her sex.

"You talk too much." Erica said in a soft voice as she placed one delicate hand in the middle of his chest and pushed him back on the bed. He offered no resistance. And when he was prone she pulled the covers off his body and moved to sit astride of his hips where he was growing by the second.

"So, you like the scarf?" she said teasing him with her words as she teased him with her body. She could feel him pressing up against her opening and she shifted just enough to let it nestle there but not make a full contact yet. "What's it worth to you?"

"What's it worth to me?" John repeated her question still holding the scarf in one hand, "How about the rest of my life? That's what it is worth to me!"

"Me too!" Erica said in a breathy whisper as she shifted her hips again but with more force this time as she engulfed him and gasped at the initial rush of intimate contact.

John sucked in his breath, dropped the scarf, grabbed her hips, and pushed her even further onto himself. Neither one of them lasted very long and they soon lay there spent and happy as the sun rose outside their little cottage in paradise. They lay together as long as they thought they could get away with and then started moving with some regret for having to leave Bahamas and return home. But that little taste of regret was far overshadowed by an expectant excitement about their future together.

****

They drove in relative silence to the airport with his hand resting on her thigh and her hand on top of his content in just being close to each other, even if it was in a car. When they arrived at the airport it was still early and they were greeted by the sight of Jamison standing outside the side door to the immigration and customs reception area with two women. As they got closer they could see that the two ladies were Sunny and Sweetness having a cup of coffee together at a beat-up looking little cabaret table and sitting on folding chairs on the side of the building in the morning sun.

John maneuvered the car into one of the empty slots beside the building and the two of them walked over to the table. Jamison stood to greet them and the two men shook hands but before either cold really speak, Erica said to Sunny, "Remember your question to me when I arrived?"

"Why yes I do, girl. I asked you if you were travelling of your own free will, but I hope you are not angry about that little joke." Sunny said looking up at the young couple.

"Well, the answer is 'no' I am not travelling of my own free will!" Erica paused for just a second for dramatic effect, then smiled broadly and continued, "If I could I would stay here forever," then sliding her arm around John's waist she added, "with this man right here!"

There were smiles of approval all around and John added, "This young lady has done me the honor of accepting my offer of marriage and I guess we are now officially engaged!"

That brought the two ladies to their feet with smiles and congratulatory hugs all round and a firm handshake and hug for Jamison and John as well.

"Then you must come back!" Sweetness added.

"We have a lovely little church here, Saint Paul's Catholic Church with a priest who gives short homilies and who is not too boring!"

That brought more smiles and laughs and then John said, "What do you think?"

Everyone paused a moment to see how Erica was going to respond, then she spoke, "Why not? Maybe a small ceremony with a few friends, then honeymoon here at the Pink Sand Cottage after a reception out at that new resort, it could work."

The only thing that broke the group's mood was the drone of a turbo-prop in the distance. Sunny and Sweetness stood and Jamison said, "Well, back to work, everyone." Then he kissed his wife on the cheek as Sunny and Sweetness went back inside to their posts at immigration and customs.

As they went back inside Jamison and John settled the car rental and Jamison said, "Would you like a quick cup of coffee?"

"Sure. In the other building?" John asked.

"No, man, you two are family now. Right here." Jamison indicated the two chairs vacated by Sunny and Sweetness. "We have time before the plane lands and they start to clear customs and need their cars." Then he pulled out his phone and punched one speed dial number and said into the instrument, "Three more cups please on the family plan."

They could see the young man starting almost immediately out the back door from the other building bringing a tray. "If you two are serious, I will give you some contact numbers to talk with the priest and to start the coordination." Jamison said.

Erica and John looked at each other then back at

Jamison and Erica spoke, "Yes, we are serious, please give us the contacts. And, you and the ladies are definitely invited!" The three were already sipping their coffee as the Brazilian made twin engine turboprop aircraft taxied off the runway and over to the parking area near the arrivals reception area.

****

Alicia and Reggie were in the middle of the stream of new arrivals making their way off the aircraft to the reception area inside the metal building. This was the first trip to the islands for both of them and they drew strength and courage to face the unknown, however unthreatening it might be, from each other. Alicia was a "military brat" and accustomed to the changes that come with some regularity to military families who move their homes and who travel around the globe. And for Reggie it was a part of that life now, in fact it was for both, but this was different.

They were not here with the knowledge, and the reassurance that knowledge brought, that there was a huge military support network in place underpinning everything they did. They were here without a net, so to speak, on their own and this was a bit intimidating. The young couple held hands, perhaps a little too tightly, and took courage from each other.

As they made their way across the tarmac their attention was drawn in different directions. Reggie saw all the little things that only someone familiar with airfield operations would spot and he was impressed. This was a bare-based, no frills operation but it was efficient and obviously well run.

Alicia on the other hand noticed that like in the states most of the workers on the airfield were black but this was different too. They weren't mostly black; they were all black. There were no white people in view anywhere . . . none.

Reggie and Alicia continued to hold hands as they made their way inside the building with the line of people coming from the little airplane.

****

So here she was in a metal building on a concrete floor standing in a line of tourists along one side of a broad red line panted on the floor facing a stern, almost regal, looking black woman. The black lady was inspecting everyone's passports and eventually waving them across the line to the other side of the large room where another stern looking black woman was inspecting their bags.

When their turn came they stood in front of this lady who raised an eyebrow as she read their names on the passports noting they used the same last name. "Are you two married?" Sunny asked.

"Yes ma'am, we are." Reggie answered and Alicia just smiled.

"Well, mister and missus, I hope you enjoy your stay on our island. Please step over to the lady at the next desk." Sunny returned their smile for just a moment then her face dropped to the stern deadpan as she called the next in line, "Next, please."

****

The rest of the process went quickly and as they stepped out into the sunny day, Jamison stood and started on his way to greet them.

"I guess we should leave and let you get back to work also." John said.

"No, no." Jamison protested, "You got a spell to

wait because they haven't even refueled the aircraft yet, just relax and let me get this couple started off. They look a little lost."

John and Erica settled back down and took another sip from their mugs as Jamison approached the other couple. "Are you looking for Jamison?" they could hear his strong voice above the background noise. They could not hear the response but they saw the look of relief from the two new arrivals.

****

With the initial introductions and the first part of the rental fees changing hands Reggie asked, "Jamison, could you give us directions to our rental?"

"Probably," Jamison responded, "I know where most of the places are here, What is it called?"

Alicia spoke up, "It is the Pink Sand Cottage, do you recognize that name?"

"Darling!" Jamison broke into a huge grin, "You two come with me a moment. I have a deal for you! And, yes I know where it is, and you must meet this other couple!"

Jamison took Alicia's bag and Reggie grabbed the other as the tall black man lead them over to the little café table on the side of the building.

"This will be your vehicle." Jamison said indicating the Jeep just a few feet away. "And Erica and John have just vacated the Pink Sand Cottage this morning." Then turning to the couple just rising from their seats, "John and Erica meet Reggie and Alicia who are the next occupants of the place you stayed."

****

"That was fortuitous!" Reggie said when they were alone in the Jeep and headed out of the airport grounds.

"I can't believe the timing. Incredible." Alicia said as she shifted in her seat to better face Reggie who was driving. "And the tips they gave were useful. I can't wait to find those diaries she mentioned and read a little about the previous occupants."

"Me too," Reggie added, "just don't forget to help me look for that Waters Store they mentioned. It's supposed to be on the way in that little town somewhere ahead."

"Can we stop for a coffee and check out that place she called Da Perk?" Alicia asked.

"Sure, I guess. As long as we can keep an eye on the Jeep and our luggage." Reggie added.

"Erica said it was in the same area as the store and that it was a safe area. So, let's give it a try, OK?"

"Sounds good, Alicia. Whatever you say. This is the honeymoon I promised you and could never deliver until now." Reggie reached over and touched her thigh.

****

As they pulled into the outskirts of a town Alicia could not help but see the many shades of blue of the water off to her right. It was turquoise, and light blue, and a light green shade and a deep blue all within a very short distance.

"Reggie, this place is beautiful." Alicia observed as she continued to stare out of the window. It so captivated her that she looked quickly to Reggie to see why he had suddenly slowed and now was making a sharp turn to the left. A moment later he had parked the Jeep and turned to look at her over the top of his glasses.

"Guess I busted the navigator check ride, huh?" Alicia said and then they both laughed. And a moment later they were seated outside the little coffee chop and sandwich bar called Da Perk.

Alicia thought it was delightful too. The tables and benches were all painted in bright primary colors and there were reds and blues and yellows all over the place. They had chosen a natural wood table with a green bench and a red bench facing each other. And, off to one side across the street the low retaining wall whose surface was painted a bright yellow. Beyond that was the little bay that came right up to the road and where some local guys were putting their little sail boats into the water.

Reggie walked inside and placed their order for a couple of fish sandwiches and a couple of lattes. Then he rejoined Alicia outside in the warm sunshine. The coffees came immediately and within ten minutes they were sampling some really excellent local fish.

"I could get used to this!" Reggie said.

"Exactly what I was thinking." Alicia chimed in.

****

They finished their sandwiches, snapped a couple of pictures and drove just a little further and found parking at the Waters Store on the other side of the street. They parked the Jeep again and made their way to the main door of the grocery store. Reggie held the door for Alicia and she went in then stopped abruptly turning to face him and said excitedly, "Reggie, it is exactly as that girl, Erica described it. Why don't you leave me alone to soak it up and get what we need. Go next door and check out the beer and wine supply."

Reggie smiled indulgently at his young pregnant wife and went next door to meet the guy in charge of their beer supply.

****

As he entered he saw several local guys leaning or sitting on cases of beer and sipping either beer or wine. They all looked at him like he was some sort of strange creature. Never shy, Reggie walked up to the older black man behind the bar and said, "You must be Johnson."

"I am, but you have me at a disadvantage, young man." Johnson Waters said and then added, "Have we met before? Do I know you?"

"No, sir, you do not know me but 'Little Johnny' said I should tell you I am his friend and you might give me a beer."

"That is a true statement!" the man behind the bar said with s flourish, "And, it will be a free beer!"

"He said I should ask for a 'cow bell,' does that make sense?" Reggie said.

"Kalik. He said you should try a Kalik." Johnson pulled a bottle out of a cooler and Reggie saw the cowbell on the label and smiled.

He took the cold beer, pulled a long draught, then set it down on the bar and said, "Well, I guess he knew what he was talking about after all."

At that the whole room laughed and Johnson explained. "Little Johnny is quite popular here and a real gentleman. He was here a week ago with a pretty girl but we haven't seen him in the past few days."

"Oh," Reggie said, "then you don't know do you?"

"Know what?" Johnson asked expressing the concern of everyone in the rom. "Is he O.K.?"

"John and Erica have gotten engaged just a day or so ago. They just left today to return home and plan their wedding."

"Well, why didn't he come and share the news?" Johnson asked slightly indignant.

"I guess he figured you would hear soon enough. You see they are coming back here for the wedding!" Reggie said, and the announcement got a round of applause from the room.

****

Suddenly the door flew open and there stood a large stern looking black woman with Alicia in tow close behind. "You see what I told you, girl. You got to watch these men every minute! That's why I made Johnson open his liquor store under my nose so I can keep an eye on him." Then turning her attention to the men, "And what is the meaning of all this noise and celebration, interrupting honest women carrying on business next door. You were being so loud that I could hardly understand this child and here is her man, the white one there, in the middle of it! Have you been corrupting this boy already?" Mrs. Waters asked with a smile on her face.

"No, dear, you don't understand," Johnson started to explain, "This man is a friend of Little Johnny and he just told us that John and the girl, Erica, are getting married!"

"That is good news!" Mrs. Waters said and turned to Alicia, "Why didn't you tell me, girl?"

"Well," Alicia said, "the best part is that they are making plans to have the wedding here on the island at the little Catholic church by the water."

Mrs. Waters turned and hugged Alicia, then she turned back to Johnson, "Well, Mr. Waters, don't you see two ladies standing in front of you here needing a beer to help celebrate?"

Johnson came up with two cold Kalik beers and started pouring them into glasses. But his wife stopped him.

"Darling, just give her a half a glass, after all she is pregnant with their first child." Mrs. Waters said.

Alicia was more than a little surprised, "How did you know? I didn't tell you that."

"I saw it in your eye girl and those hips of yours so young and trim have never given birth, but don't worry, you'll widen nicely just like I did when the time comes."

****

18. REGGIE & ALICIA: AT THE COTTAGE

They had a pleasant time at the impromptu celebration for half an hour or so then managed to extract themselves from the group. They loaded the food and the beer into the back of the Jeep and headed on to the cottage. On the drive to the end of the paved road, Alicia asked Reggie, "Do you suppose she's right? That my hips will get a big as hers?"

"Baby, I don't think so!" Reggie said without hesitation. "My guess is that Mrs. Waters never had hips as sexy as yours and that she hasn't done much exercise in the past forty years or so. Just relax and don't worry about it!"

Alicia smiled and hugged his arm, but then he added, "Besides Johnson still loves her and I suppose that even if you did get as broad as she is I would still love you too."

Alicia let go of his arm and hit him on the shoulder, "You were doing just fine there for a minute, white boy, but you blew it." Then with a smile competing with a fake frown, "This cottage better have a couch so you'll have someplace to sleep tonight!"

****

Then a few minutes later, "Are you sure we have the right road?" Alicia asked as they left the paved road.

"Well, I think so based on what John said at the airport. But this thing looks more like two ruts in a jungle than a road." Reggie answered. "But I'm going for it."

"I don't know," Alicia said softly, "I don't like the way those vines and that vegetation are closing in on

172

the road ahead." Alicia said sounding a little more concerned.

"Come on, baby, where's your spirit of adventure?" Reggie said trying to take her mind off the road.

"My 'spirit of adventure' is how a respectable black girl like me from a good family wound up married to a white boy lost in a jungle in a foreign country surrounded by black folk who look like me but with whom I have absolutely nothing in common!" Alicia replied but with a weak smile.

He could tell she took the bait in the conversation to take her mind off the situation that really did have her a little worried. Doing a quick assessment he reasoned that he had never heard of an insurgency in the Bahamas and had never heard of any "man eating beasts" and these people did make a lot of their money from tourists so they were probably safe. Of course he told her none of this because that would just lead down a never ending path of explanations and challenges of every assumption he had just made.

Instead, he said, "Alicia, that wasn't much of a leap of faith down the adventurous highway! You knew I was an Air Force NCO when we met because I was wearing my uniform. You knew I was a nice guy because I changed your tire in a parking lot." She tried to interrupt but he held up a hand so she let him continue.

"And, you knew your old man was a retired Master Sergeant who would kick my butt if I ever did anything to endanger his little girl. So, you tell me again about your adventurous spirit!"

Alicia took a deep breath but held it stopping short

as the road widened and she could see the beautiful houses lining the road from time to time facing out onto the water. Instead of replying to his last she just reached over and patted his leg and said, "See, I told you everything was going to be alright, this is perfect!"

Reggie did the only thing he could do, he shook his head and laughed a little laugh, smiling at her. He was happy to see she was smiling back at him again. And, he said a little silent prayer to his Guardian Angel because they were on the right road and he knew if they had really been lost he never would have heard the end of it.

****

A little further down the road with its wide spots for cars to pass and for the homes that were nestled in the midst of intense vegetation they came to it. The owners house was on the right side of the road and it was very large but it was also obviously closed for the time being. On the left was a wood frame structure with pink painted wood siding and white lattice work around the bottom and a parking place designated by a hand made sign on a short pole identifying the Pink Sand Cottage.

The parking place was a small clearing nestled among the palm trees with odd shaped large concrete tiles defining a path through the palm trees. On the path along the side of the house some of the concrete tiles were heart shaped and some were circles and some were square. And the path to the back was defined by hexagon concrete tiles leading to six wooden steps up to the back door and a small porch.

The car was barely parked before Alicia had jumped out, tiptoed along the path with Reggie in tow

174

and she was headed along the side of the house through the dense palm trees and toward the water. Reggie caught up with her as they saw together a large platform slightly raised off to the right side with folding lounge chairs for sunning. It was large and of two levels so that several chairs would fit with ease.

To the left was a small porch running along the length of the house and framing the front door. But the real delight came from the view straight ahead. They were on top of a berm of maybe eight or ten feet with a sharp drop to the beach. Someone had planted sea lettuce on the berm to control erosion and it had thrived, and the colors were striking. The sea lettuce was bright green and lush looking and covered the entire berm and almost up to the little porch on the front of the house.

The palm trees were mature and lush and there were pretty red and purple flowers that made a perfect accent. And then there was the beach – it really was pink! There was a light pink tint to the entire thing and the play of the sun on the water shifting shades of blue, aqua, green and even a deep blue on the horizon that made the effect perfect. And, far out near the horizon was a cruise ship making its transit.

Alicia took it all in in a second and then turned to Reggie. He looked down into her eyes and she grabbed his head in her hands and pulled his face down to hers and their lips met. She kissed him long and lovingly. When the kiss ended, Alicia pressed her face to is chest and said, "Thank you, baby, this is perfect!"

"Now that you are happy, it is indeed perfect." Reggie responded and held her for a long moment as they stood there alone in the world with the warm sun and the gentle breeze. Caressing them.

****

"But, as nice as this is, I think I better get the bags inside." Reggie said as they broke the embrace.

"Do you need some help?" Alicia asked.

"No, actually, if you could open the place up I can get the bags up." Reggie replied and they took off to their respective tasks.

Alicia unlocked the back door and walked into the small but efficient kitchen. The kitchen area was separated from the rest of the one very large room by a rattan tiki-style bar. She saw that just beyond the bar was a comfortable sitting area and a bed on the far side. The bed was positioned so you would awake in the morning looking at the view. This was well thought out she said to herself.

She had just opened the front door onto the narrow porch as Reggie made it up the stairs with the first bag. "Wow, I like this!" he said.

"I was just thinking the same thing." Alicia responded ad then added, "I love it! It's so cute and everything is functional and comfortable."

They unpacked the bags together negotiating drawer space and beginning to settle into a comfortable rhythm. As they were finishing, she turned to Reggie and said, "Tell me again about my sexy hips and I might let you off the couch and back onto the bed."

Reggie pulled her close and began to unbutton her pants to slide them over her hips, "I need to examine the evidence first." He said playfully as he peeled the jeans over her hips, catching the top of her panties as his hands slid past them. Within seconds she was standing there with her clothing in a heap on the floor around her ankles.

Alicia stepped out of the clothes, first with one foot, then with the other and stood inches from his face. Her feet were shoulder width apart with her hands on her hips. "Well?" she said.

"Baby, you are without a doubt the sexiest woman I have ever seen!" Reggie said as his breath came a little faster.

"You talk way too much." Alicia said playfully as she pushed him back n the couch and stepped astride his lap.

In a matter of minutes they were lost in each other's bodies and eventually made their way to the bed.

****

They made love repeatedly the way young people do as if they are afraid there will never be another chance. The urgency in their love making was palpable and in the end they were both exhausted, so they slept.

****

When he woke it was to the sound of the shower going in the little bathroom on the other side of the wall. A moment later while he was still stretching, she came out of the bathroom and padded across the floor barefoot to retrieve her panties from a drawer in the chest. He watched her and smiled.

"What are you smiling at, mister?" she said pulling the panties up over her hips. "You haven't earned the bed yet for the night, that was just a trial run to see if you are worth my time!" she teased.

Reggie was out of the bed in one swift movement, sweeping her up into his arms and into the air like a child. He held her there a second, then he kissed her and asked, "And, did I pass the test?"

"Oh, baby, you passed the test when you asked me if you could change my tire that day in the parking lot at the mall." With that Alicia put her arms around his neck and kissed him again.

"Now, put me down and get a quick shower and let's go outside, OK?"

"Sounds good to me!" Reggie said as he moved the arm under her knees and gently released her legs so she could stand.

****

A few minutes later he came out to the little porch on the front of the cottage and was struck by the contrast of her caramel skin and the white bikini and the little bulge starting to show in her midsection. This was his wife, indeed this was his life and here they were on an island paradise and awaiting their first child. He realized he had so much for which to be thankful.

Reggie felt he had the perfect life!

Alicia turned a second later and saw him just standing there looking at her and the scenery and the setting with a strange look on his face. "Everything O.K. Reggie? Something wrong? You look like you have just seen a ghost." Alicia prodded him.

"In a way, I have," he answered, "I have just seen a flash of the rest of our lives and I like it. I like it a lot."

"Tell me about it." Alicia said.

"I see you and me and three kids. Actually, grandkids," he corrected himself. Then continuing as she fell silent, "And you are as pretty and as trim as ever."

Alicia smiled into his eyes and saw the love then she saw a glimmer of something else.

"Although, I gotta' admit, in this vision your hips did get a little bigger . . ."

"You are not even getting the couch tonight," she started, "enjoy this porch right here because I am locking you out."

Reggie reached out to her but she pulled away and continued her rant, "You are about the dumbest white boy I have ever met and you don't know when to shut up and just let things happen. I should have listened to my aunt when she told me . . ."

She couldn't talk now because his lips were on hers, and through the kiss he said, "You know I am kidding and you know you are the most beautiful woman I have ever seen and I want to spend the rest of our lives together, . . ."

"You doin' fine right now so you better stop talking before you say something else dumb." And, with that she kissed him back.

"Now, grab that beach bag and let's go for a walk."

****

Reggie looked to his right then pointed to the wooden deck sunning platform to the side of the house where the reclining beach chairs were set on either side of a little table. "Can't we just go over there and sit between the palm trees and get some sun?"

His voice trailed off as Alicia gave him one of those looks that told him to shut up and grab the bag because they were going for a walk on the beach.

She led the way to the wooden steps leading down to the beach with him in tow with a beach bag of undefined contents over his shoulder. But they only got half the way down the wooden stairs when they both stopped and just took in the view.

Reggie and Alicia were perched on the wooden steps about half the way down the berm with a veritable wall of bright green sea lettuce behind them.

But, directly ahead of them was an expanse of pink tinted sand as far as the eye could see. It was littered occasionally by a thin line of flotsam left behind by the receding tide. It seemed to give a counterpoint of sorts to the fine pink sand.

Beyond the sand there was the gentle lap of aqua-shaded water, mixed with light blue water, and the dark blue water on the horizon. In the distance the sun was bright but somehow not hot. Maybe that was because of the light wind blowing along the beach.

"Wow, would you look at that." Alicia said over her shoulder to Reggie, "This really is the perfect place for a delayed honeymoon."

"That's not all," Reggie added, "look down, baby. See any footprints?"

Alicia literally ran down the rest of the steps jumping off the last one to land with both feet like a child on the pristine sand. "No! There are no footprints except mine!" she said with a note of excitement, "It's like our own private beach! Nobody here but us, and I love it."

Reggie followed her down and stood beside her holding her hand with one of his hands and the beach bag with the other. "Look up there, Alicia, the cottage is so pretty with that pink and white color scheme and the bright green berm and the pink sand and the water; I don't think I ever want to leave."

Alicia leaned against him, "I know," she said, "I know."

****

They strolled and chatted along the beach noting that the one big green house near theirs was empty at present and that the next nearest place was about a quarter mile away. This really was their private beach for the next week.

Eventually they turned back and as they approached the house Reggie said, "Baby, can we talk about something serious for a minute?"

"That sounds ominous, but sure, honey, what's on your mind?" Alicia responded.

"So, I'm thinking about what comes next . . ." Reggie started but Alicia cut him off.

"What do you mean, what comes next?" Alicia had a little edge to her voice that Reggie did not understand at first, but which became clear quickly, "We leave this place in a week and go home and I have a baby and we talk about this to our friends until they are sick of hearing about it."

Reggie pulled closer and put his arms around her shoulders, "Actually, that's exactly what I want to talk about. Please hear me out." He could feel her go tense but she didn't say anything and he continued. "The baby will change our life and that is a good thing. But, the money is not going to go as far as it did before, even with the promotion pay raise." He felt her shoulders tense again.

"We need a way to increase our income because cutting expenses is only going to go so far. . ."

"Will you get to the point!" Alicia cut him of again. "I'm about to have a panic attack here and I'm feeling really vulnerable! So, just say it!"

"Panic attack? About what?" Reggie asked with real concern in his voice.

"Well, I am standing here pregnant and with very few options and you are talking about unspecified changes, and the expenses about to come at us, and life changing, and I'm thinking you are building up to dumping me or telling me you want 'out'! That's why I'm feeling a little vulnerable right now! So, spit it out, Reggie."

"You are the craziest little black girl I have ever known!" Reggie said suppressing a laugh.

"What's so funny, Reggie?" Alicia demanded.

"Baby, I'm trying to ask you for your support to go for Officer Training School." Reggie said.

"What?" Alicia blurted out, but Reggie felt the tension leave her shoulders even as she slid out from under is arm and turned to face him.

"Alicia, I am within a couple of courses of finishing my Bachelors' Degree. It will take more time away from us, but I can push and finish everything in the next semester, before the baby comes," he inserted, "and have time to apply for the next cycle."

Alicia looked up into his eyes and Reggie saw the relief and the love in her eyes, "Yes, I can support that, honey, in fact I can probably support it better now than after the baby comes." Then in a flash of realization she added, "But how long will you be gone for OTS?"

"Baby, this is OTS not basic training. It happens right here at Maxwell Air Force Base in Montgomery. The course is about nine and a half weeks, say ten weeks with the paperwork and processing. So, if there is a crisis I can be with you in a matter of minutes, literally. And your parents are right here too so you won't exactly be alone."

"That's true, I better go talk to mom and dad . . ."

"Oh, I already have, they like the idea." Reggie said smiling.

Alicia rankled up a bit and said, "Reggie, you really are the dumbest white boy I ever met. You are also the dumbest white boy I ever fell in love with! Why didn't you talk to me first?"

Reggie spoke slowly obviously choosing his words carefully, "Baby, it's not like that. I talked with your dad about a career officer track versus a career NCO track and he gave me solid advice including saying he might have done the same thing if times had been different for him and your mom."

"I didn't realize that." Alicia said in all sincerity.

Reggie continued, "That's when your mom came into the room. I suspect she was listening from another room . . ."

"Ya, think?" Alicia asked a bit sarcastically.

Reggie let it go and continued, ". . . anyway she jumped in as a volunteer to help you with the new baby while I am at OTS, assuming I can get accepted. Which, by the way I am optimistic about. My Colonel said he would back me and your dad said he knew a retired General who would talk to me and might give me a recommendation."

"And what if I had said, 'no'?" Alicia asked.

"Well then we wouldn't have gotten this far in the conversation." Reggie answered.

"I still haven't said 'yes'." Alicia pointed out.

"And, you haven't said no either. Don't you see, baby, that's why I wanted to present you with a well thought out realistic option, not just a pipe dream."

Alicia didn't say a word but she did hug him around the waist and rest her head on his chest.

"So, is that a yes?" Reggie asked over the top of her head.

"Don't rush me. I have to get used to the idea and the whole sequence of events, including my mom being in the middle of my life for about three months." Alicia said as they started up the wooden steps to the Pink Sand Cottage.

"We can talk some more later." She added but he could see she was starting to smile.

****

19. JOHN & ERICA: AT MARINA HOTEL

"Well that was fortunate!" John said as they left the registration desk and made their way to the bank of elevators. "I guess they stay pretty full here this time of year. Did you see the look on his face when I asked to extend the reservation?"

"Yeah," Erica said, "he looked like he was in pain or something."

"Then when he came back and said there had been a cancellation, I was ecstatic." John said, "I was ready to start calling the other hotels in town." Then interrupting himself, "Ah, this is our floor." And he held the door with his foot while they maneuvered their bags out of the elevator.

Well, bags would have been an exaggeration, they still had just the two backpacks and that was it! When Erica cleared the door, John handed her the electronic key and reached over and took her backpack too.

It was a short walk down the hall to their door and Erica slid the key card into the slot and opened the door. John followed her in and then they both stopped. As they saw the room open up n front of them. After a minute Erica said, "Are we in the right room?"

"This place is huge!" John responded as he stood there holding the two backpacks.

Erica maneuvered around him and went back to the door. She opened it and checking the room number again. "Yep, this is ours." She said flatly.

They moved into the rest of the three room suite together and almost jumped when the phone on the desk rang. John picked it up, "Hello." He said.

The small speaker of the instrument was loud

enough the Erica could hear the tinny voice say, "I trust the room is alright." The disembodied voice said.

"Yes. It is very nice but this is not what we were expecting, thank you." John replied.

"Well," the metallic voice said again, "my manager was standing behind you two as you waited and heard you talking about your engagement. This is his idea. Your room is one of our bridal suites and we hope you will consider using us for your honeymoon."

"Oh, absolutely!" Erica said over his shoulder.

John added, "You heard the lady, we will certainly consider this for our honeymoon." They ended the call and John turned to take Erica into his arms. They held each other a long time and it didn't really matter where they were because the rest of the world just seemed to fade away for a few minutes.

****

As they broke the embrace after what seemed like hours John looked down into her eyes and asked, "Do you still have that scarf you bought here a week ago?"

Erica looked up at him and said playfully, "Maybe." And with that she grabbed her backpack and walked into the bedroom closing the door behind herself.

A moment later John heard the bath water running as he went over to the mini-bar and pulled out a small bottle of rum and a coke and made himself a stiff drink. He wandered out onto the balcony of the suite and sipped the drink for several minutes just letting reality sink in.

He was about to get married to the most beautiful and exciting woman he had ever met. "Wow" he said to himself, my life is suddenly getting very, very good.

He toasted himself, then checked his watch. She had been in there about ten minutes.

John went back to the mini-bar and opened a bottle of cabernet sauvignon, poured it into the hotel wine glass and carried it into the bedroom area. Her clothes were dumped onto the bed and she had the scarf laid out as well, he noticed as he moved towards the open door of the bathroom. He looked over at her soaking in a steamy tub, held out the glass of wine and said, "Would the lady like a glass of wine?"

Erica sat forward raising her breasts out of the water and said, somewhat coyly, "The lady would indeed like a glass of wine. That would be very nice."

John stepped forward and handed her the glass of deep crimson liquid. Erica accepted the drink, sipped it and nodded appreciatively. Then with a flick of her small hand she waved him away saying, "You may go."

John smiled to himself and backed out of the bathroom. When he crossed the threshold of the bedroom he turned and strolled back out to the sitting room and onto the balcony with his rum and coke. He returned to his seat and watched the light fade in the evening sky.

It wasn't long and it was definitely worth the wait. He became aware of her approach as the light clicked off in the sitting room behind him. He turned around to see her come out onto the balcony barefooted and naked except for the scarf tied at her waist. It took his breath away for a second.

Erica, his girlfriend and his future wife, was even more beautiful than when he had first seen her wearing just this scarf. Wow, had it really been such a short time ago, in this same hotel?

She padded over to him across the concrete of the balcony and extended her hand to him. He started to speak but she cut him off with a raised finger of her free hand and said, "You talk too much."

John stood and let her lead him back inside the suite, across the lush carpet of the sitting rom and into the bedroom. Then he stood there as she slowly undressed him. He could smell the lavender of her shampoo and the soft floral touch of her perfume.

As he stepped out of his pants she placed one small hand in the middle of his chest and pushed him gently back onto the bed. He sat down and moved up to the head of the bed as she came up beside him. Erica stood there a moment as she pulled the knot at her waist and the scarf fell to the floor.

She came to him and kissed his chest and as she slid down the length of him he cold feel her nipples brush against his skin. When her hands got a little lower she found he was ready and without a word she raised one leg to straddle him.

She was ready too and his entry was smooth and silky and the warmth of her engulfed him. She could feel the stiffness and the pleasant sensation of the hair rubbing together almost teasing their most sensitive spots.

They lost the rest of the world as they became one together. They moved with wanton abandon one minute, then with a more quiet, almost gentle, movement the next minute. She moved from one set of motions to the other easily sensing when he might be about to release and changed so they could go longer and then changing yet again.

Finally he arched his back and she felt him explode

inside of her as his own hot fluids mixed with hers and she tensed and came a second later and then fell against his chest. They lay there spent in a tangle of arms and legs and bedclothes and luxuriated in each other.

And then they slept.

****

The next morning she heard his shower and decided to join him and they soaped each other and dried each other when the shower was done. Erica looked up at him in an inquiring way but he just said, "I have already ordered room service so throw on a robe and let's discuss that option after a little food, shall we?"

Erica pouted playfully. "Well if we have to." And as she tied her robe there was a knock at the door. By the time she came out of the bathroom and through the bedroom John had tipped the hotel employee and was uncovering the small table of food they had rolled into the sitting room.

Beyond the balcony she could see a perfect sky and the promise of a warm sunny day ahead. Erica smiled and her face beamed with satisfaction. She sat and picked up a cup of coffee that he offered, "So, John, what is on your mind this morning?"

"Well, eventually, I want to make love with you and just hold you in my arms." John started.

"Eventually?" Erica said encouraging him to continue and to clarify.

"Baby, first we have to make this an 'official' engagement," he said as he reached over and plucked a piece of paper off the table near the sofa. Then he continued, "and have here a list of half a dozen reputable jewelry stores accessible by taxi."

"John, we don't have to do this." Erica started but John cut her off. "Yes, baby, we do have to do this. I don't want some other guy to get the wrong idea. I want the world to know you are spoken for!"

She started to speak but he held up a finger to quiet here, "And," he continued but in a softer voice, "when you have the ring on your finger we want to call your family and mine and break the news to them. I don't know about your mother but I know mine! And if we skip too many steps there will be a serious reckoning in our future!" he said sternly but with a smile creeping into the corners of his mouth.

This time it was Erica's turn to be serious, "John, you are right about calling our mothers but I don't want to start our life together weighed down with a lot of debt. Are you sure you want to do this right now?"

"Baby, who said anything about debt. You do remember that I am a banker, right? I might be a junior banker but I make a good salary and I do not have any really bad habits so I save a hefty percentage of my income every pay period."

He continued, "I have already made contact with the senior manager of our local branch here and have set up things so that when you find the ring you want, we can literally transfer the money from my account into theirs."

Erica stood and hugged him then reached up and kissed him, "Then I guess I better get ready to do some serious shopping this morning." With that she padded away from him across the carpet loosening her robe as she went and letting it fall to the floor as she crossed into the bedroom."

John got the clue and immediately followed her

into the bedroom. "Well, we do have a few minutes he said." As there was a bouncing sound from the bed.

****

At the third store they entered she found the perfect ring. She saw a beautiful ring of traditional yellow gold with a diamond setting that was elegant and eye-catching without being too flashy. It was a two ring set with the wedding band and the diamond engagement ring and a matching man's wedding band. She tried it on and her face lit up and John could see this would be the one.

In fact John saw everything he needed to see in a second. He saw the look on her face the light in her eyes and the smile she gave him. She was admiring the ring, the way it looked on her hand and asking with her eyes if it was O.K.

In a glance John saw the price tag, expensive but not prohibitive, and he saw a money transfer from the technical perspective of how long it would take and most importantly he saw the look in her eyes. John took her hands in is and looked down into her eyes, "Is this the one?" he asked quietly.

"Yes," she said excitedly and then started to ask, "but is it too . . ."

He stopped her with a finger to her lips shushing her. "Let me talk with the manager and we can close this today."

He tried to turn to the store manager but she grabbed his neck and gave him a long hug first. When he finally extricated himself he asked the sales rep if he could talk to the general manager.

The sales rep secured the ring and then led them into the back of the store to see the manager. John explained what he had in mind and within minutes he and the manager were with the finance officer in front of a computer while she drank a cup of coffee the sales rep had offered her.

A few minutes later John joined her in the front of the store with a cup of his own. They all made small talk until about half an hour later when the manager came out from the back and asked when the lady would like to take delivery of her rings.

****

It was funny, she told herself, later at the hotel as she soaked in a hot tub in the bridal suite. She had not thought this would make a difference but it did. She felt different about herself and about them, even though the only thing that had changed from this morning was a ring on her finger. Somehow it made the phone call to their mothers a lot easier and more fun. After all, this was an official engagement and she had to admit she liked the feel of that.

****

20. REGGIE & ALICIA: PACKING TO LEAVE BUT WITH PLANS TO RETURN

Reggie and Alicia were starting to pack their few essential travel items but neither one was moving too quickly. They really were not in much of a hurry to leave this wonderful place. They had walked on the beach, and had morning coffee on the front porch.

They had snuggled on the couch watching an old movie over the satellite connection on the little flat screen TV up in the corner of the room over the bed when it had rained. Instinctively they snuggled closer half watching the old movie and half listening to the patter of the rain outside as the sun disappeared into the water peeking occasionally through the clouds.

"Promise me we'll come back." Alicia said as she nuzzled against Reggie's chest. "I mean, I know it will be a few years because of the baby and your plans for OTS and all, but just promise we will come back here again, OK?"

"Baby, I was thinking the same thing. I mean three years seems about right. Our child will be about three years old more or less and able to be left with a family member and I should be done with my studies, OTS and getting settled into a billet as a Lieutenant. Is that about what you are thinking?"

"Yeah," she replied noncommittally, "that's part of what I was thinking, But I was also thinking, wow, my baby's daddy is going to be an officer. And then I was thinking I want to make love to you one more time before we have to go in the morning."

"Uh, Baby, I'm very good with all of that." Reggie said enthusiastically.

"But I want to do it right now in the dark, in the rain on the beach!" Alicia said as she stood pulling her T-shirt off over her head and dropping her shorts onto the floor of the cottage.

Reggie stood and did the same thing and they half ran half walked out the front door, across the little porch and down the stairs to the beech. They could almost see were they were between the last of the sun's rays and occasional flash of lightening in the distance filtering between the clouds.

When they got to the beach Alicia turned and placed a small caramel hand on his chest and stopped him. Then she steadied herself and sank down to her knees and he felt the warmth and passion in her mouth but it didn't last long as he sprang to life.

She stood and pushed lightly against his chest indicating he should lie down on his back. He did so and before he could say a word she was over his hips and lowering herself onto him. This time she clearly wanted to be in charge and he went with it. She demanded and he responded and they moved as one.

****

They lay together breathing heavy and holding each other on the sand for several minutes. Then the sprinkle of rain turned into a real downpour and they ran back up the steps and onto the porch laughing and holding hands like a couple of kids.

They stood there a moment naked and alone in the world covered by the night. She wrapped her arms against his trim hard midsection and he placed one long muscled arm around her shoulders and they watched the rain fall and listened to the wind as it started to pick up.

Finally Alicia spoke, "Now will you promise me

we will return some day?"

"Girl," he said dragging out the word, "you give me time to go by the bank and borrow some money and we can come back here next week after that little experience!" They both laughed and hugged and went inside out of the weather.

****

The next morning they threw their few possessions into the bags and headed to the airport. As they got to the start of the paved road Alicia said, "Daddy told me you were a 'keeper' and he was right."

"When did he tell you that?" Reggie asked veering to miss a truck.

"That first night when you came to meet him wearing your uniform." She responded.

"He did, huh?" Reggie tugged at the thread of conversation.

"Yes he did. And he told me not to mess this one up because you were a step up from the guys I usually brought home." She said smiling over at him.

"Uh-huh, and just how many guys was it you brought home?" he pressed the point.

"Maybe one or two." She said coyly.

"Yeah, well he told me something too just before the wedding." Reggie baited her.

"What was that?" Alicia took the bait.

"Well I don't know if he would want me to share that or not, baby." Reggie teased her.

"Reginald," she used his Christian name so he would know she was serious, "What did he tell you before the wedding?"

"He looked me in the eye and told me that 'all sales are final' and I could not return you."

Alicia hit him on the arm with a small brown fist, "He did not!" she said, with indignation in her voice.

"No, he didn't. He told me you were his baby girl and I had better treat you right or there would be hell to pay." Reggie said.

"That, I believe." Alicia said with a smile in her voice.

****

There was a brief silence and then Alicia spoke again, "He was right, baby, you are a keeper. And, you know what else," and before he could answer she pushed ahead, "you are going to excel at OTS and be the best young officer they have ever seen. I gotta' tell you, I was pretty happy with our life before we left on this trip but I am down right ecstatic now!"

"Baby, I am going to make you proud and our family will be the model for all those recruiting posters – beautiful home, beautiful wife, beautiful baby, and beautiful Lieutenant . . ."

"See," she said, "there you go again! You were doing great until that last bit. I swear you are about the dumbest white boy I have ever met." There was a laugh in her voice and when he looked over she was smiling and actually glowing.

I am one lucky man he thought to himself; no make that one 'blessed man.' This is a blessing that I have done nothing to earn and I do thank God.

****

At the airport Jamison was waiting and took them over to the little café table as they settled the bill for the rental car and handed over the keys.

Jamison waved a young boy over and offered them a cup of coffee that they accepted and they all sat for a moment.

"So, how was your visit?" Jamison asked Alicia.

"It was wonderful and we are coming back in a couple of years, as soon as the baby is old enough to be left with someone." Alicia said with a smile.

"Oh, I see. Like a little 'get away' for new mom and dad?" Jamison turned to Reggie as he framed this question.

"Exactly." Reggie answered, "Of all the vacation spots I can think of the people and the area are outstanding. And that little rain storm last night was even charming in its own special way." He looked over at Alicia.

She smiled sweetly at him but her eyes warmed him not to go any further in this conversation. After a moment Jamison said, "I am glad you had a good time and want to return. I would look forward to seeing you again some day soon."

They both just looked at Jamison a moment until Reggie spoke, "Jamison, I believe you mean that. This place really is special and you have a wonderful little island world here. Yes, it is very likely my wife and I will be back. This is a place to make memories and to enjoy memories."

With that they stood, shook hands and headed into the departure area of the large metal building.

****

EPILOGUE

SAMANTHA: ONE YEAR LATER

John spotted her first and when Erica looked to see what had caught his attention she said, "She looks familiar. Do we know her?"

****

Samantha looked regal in an understated way. She was tall and slim in a tailored linen suit with large dark glasses obscuring the largest part of her face. And, the hat, which matched the suit in color and material, was pulled at an angle to shield her from the sun. Samantha walked through the crowded airport lobby looking like someone who did not want to be bothered with the small details. If the truth be known this was a part of her defense mechanism and she had retreated from the world until this task was complete.

Arthur would have said, "I am on a mission" she mused to herself. Arthur, the former military officer, and Arthur her husband, and Arthur the best man she had ever known, would have called this a mission not a task.

A task, he would have said, was just something you did because you had to do it. On the other hand a mission was something you took on voluntarily and it had an objective to be accomplished and a plan for its accomplishment. Yes, a mission was part of some larger goal or over riding objective and vision.

So Samantha kept putting one foot in front of the other and sighed, because Arthur was not here and would never be here again. And, she would be Arthur's widow, or maybe - she stopped. She did not know what she would be. She still owned her business and to those who depended on her she would still be the "boss." She owned the house and to her neighbors she would be the lady in the big brick house. But so much of her life had been defined by the relationship they had shared and now he was gone. She would be alone. Ultimately, that's what she would be – alone.

She could busy herself with work and neighbors and occasional fundraisers or volunteer work with the church but she would be alone at night with her memories. She just thanked God for the memories of their time together because it had been glorious.

****

Then she realized she had better focus because she was at the ticket counter.

"Yes, ma'am, can I help you?" the ticket agent said.

"Yes," Samantha replied, "I have a reservation for the next flight to Governor's Harbour. Here is my identification, my passport, and my ticket number." Samantha said as she passed over the documents.

After a few moments, "Yes, ma'am, everything seems to be in order. Here are your boarding pass and your documents back. Please go up the stairs at the end of this concourse and through security and you will find the departure gate. Hope you enjoy your visit to Bahamas."

"Thank you." Was all that Samantha said to the overly friendly desk clerk for Silver Airlines. She turned away pulling her one roll-along carry-on bag which she knew would not fit into the overhead and that she would have to leave at the aircraft as she boarded.

****

Samantha settled into the seat and looked out the window lost in her thoughts. So he had given her one last "mission" and she knew that it was in part just to give her something to do to take her mind off the fact that he was no longer there with her.

Arthur wanted a wake, but not a wake in Columbia, South Carolina among their friends and neighbors, oh no he wanted a wake in Eleuthra among their adopted friends from the Island. So here she was on a plane alone figuring out how this would be done.

The priest in Columbia had been adamant that the ashes were to be interred, not spread to the four winds and that the interment was to take place as soon after the funeral service as possible. So the urn was placed into their niche in the columbarium where a space waited for her own urn to be placed at some future date.

So she did not even have the ashes with her. Art had shown her the articles about the history of Irish wakes ending with the casket being lowered into the earth and the shovels being placed in the form of a cross on top of the grave at the end.

She got the idea, well enough but the body was already cremated and in its resting place and there was nothing to lower into the ground to mark the end of the ceremony. The more she grappled with the details the more sure she was that this was just his way of taking her mind off of the fact that he was now gone.

****

Traditional Irish wakes ran the gamut from deep and profound grieving for the deceased to boisterous good times with free flowing adult beverages and song. Mind you none of this was meant as a disrespect for the deceased but it was rather a celebration to his or her life and tribute to their having been among the living for as long as they were. In fact the older the person the more profound the celebrations and mourning. It was the result of some sort of melding of the pagan Irish customs and the Christian funeral services. No doubt this would be a toned down affair since it was certainly not going to go on for days and in fact it would likely only last a few hours at most.

****

As she sat there on the little plane lost in her thoughts, John and Erica came down the aisle and sat beside her.

"Excuse me, ma'am," John started, "but I think I know you."

Samantha looked up not fully registering what he was saying. "I beg your pardon." She said.

"I'm sorry to interrupt you. My name is John and this is Erica. I think I met you at that little cottage on Eleuthra several years ago. I was part of a diving group and a tall ex-Army guy was kind enough to let me come up and chat. I believe his name is Art . . ."

"Was." Sam interrupted. "His name was Art and he has only recently passed away."

"I am so sorry," John said as Erica let a tear escape her eyes. "I had no idea." Then as if by way of explanation he added, "I had been telling my wife, Erica, about that chance meeting and your kindness to me that led us to rent the same cottage. In fact we are staying there this trip."

As the engines began to start their run-up further conversation was not practical. But Sam did manage to say, "I will be in town at one of the hotels for a few days. Perhaps we can talk again."

****

As the little plane made its way towards its destination at Governor's Harbour she was once again lost in her thoughts. Art had wanted an Irish wake. So Sam had dutifully done her research.

There would be clay pipes, tobacco, snuff and candles and every male visitor was expected to at least take a puff because the smoke helped to keep the evil spirits away. The deceased might even have a pipe on his chest.

The body would not be left alone and there would be no weeping our verbal mourning until the body was prepared, otherwise one might attract evil spirits to the occasion. When the preparations were complete the crying would begin not before because crying might attract evil spirits who could take the soul of the departed.

Well she had already flunked that part of her mission. In fact everyone who had been at the church service had flunked that part. Art had been loved in their community back home and he was already being missed. Every time she saw someone who had known him they told her so. Maybe that was a part of why he had asked me to do this, she thought.

Maybe he had instinctively known this, and had just wanted to get her away from all the sadness for a while. That would have been just like him, she thought.

Her mind wandered back to the wake. At the end of an Irish wake, the deceased would be laid into the casket and it would be lowered into the ground. Then the soil of Ireland would be spread on top of the coffin with the shovels laid in the pattern of a cross.

Just as she focused again on that sad symbol of the

crossed shovels on top of the fresh grave the plane touched down.

****

As the little plane made its landing at Governor's Harbor she was back to her original thoughts. How was she going to pull this off? It's a good thing Jeanie is here with me on this mission, she said to herself.

Jeanie was Art's daughter from his first marriage and she had already been a young adult when Art and Sam met. The two women had bonded over their common love of the man; loving wife and devoted daughter. She had flown in yesterday and they were sharing a room at one of the local hotels for a couple of days. In truth neither woman wanted to be alone right now.

As she made her way through the immigration and customs process at Governor's Harbour, Sunny was waiting at the immigration counter and Sweetness was behind the customs table. Sam could see Jeanie near the door standing beside Jamison and it was almost like coming home to a family reception.

****

Erica leaned in closer to Samantha. "Sam, may I call you that?" Erica asked, and then continued without waiting for an answer. "Look, this is a tough time for you, we know, but we will be here all week and if you need anything, including a place to sit and think, just call." With that she handed Samantha a piece of paper with their cell phone numbers written on it.

Sam nodded and dropped the folded piece of paper into her purse as Erica added, "Besides John is very, very good at organizing and making things happen so if you have any issues at all please feel free to call. He

203

knows you and I already feel like I do . . ."

John butted into the conversation trying to make this less awkward as the line started to move forward, "What Erica is trying to say is if you need anything at all we are here for you. Without you and Art we would not have come to the Pink Sand Cottage in the first place and that is where I proposed to Erica."

Sam nodded her appreciation and thanks for their offer and said a soft, "Thanks to you both."

****

Just then the door behind Jamison opened and Johnson Waters held the door open for his wife Gladys, who everyone called "Mom," to enter. Samantha waved at them and shifted her attention to the entry and customs process.

****

"Excuse me everyone," Sunny said in a loud voice and everyone turned to look at her. "Thank you," she continued, "I would like to take these three people first." Sunny indicated Samantha along with Erica and John. "This is a special situation and I would like your cooperation."

Everyone in the line shrugged and stepped to one side to let them move to the front of the line. The checks were quick and cursory and as they stepped across the red line painted on the concrete floor that marked "entry" into The Bahamas, Sweetness came around the customs table and gave them each a hug.

Jamison and Johnson grabbed the luggage and moved the group quickly out into the fresh air as Sweetness returned to her station. Sunny could be heard saying "Thank you for your cooperation and patience," as she took the passports of the next couple in line.

****

Outside on the sidewalk after the hugs and greetings were exchanged, John, true to form took control of the group conversation. "Everyone, I think there has been some confusion." As they looked to him he continued, "Samantha is not traveling with Erica and me. We just happened to be on the same plane. I am sure you are here for her and we will excuse ourselves . . ."

This time it was Sam who spoke, "John, before you do, allow me to introduce Jeanie." Then as the younger woman stepped forward, "Jeanie is Arthur's daughter and one of my closest friends. Jeanie, this is John and his wife Erica. I have just met Erica and already feel like I know her."

Erica reached out to touch Samantha's arm as Sam continued, "John met Art and me a few years ago at that little cottage in all the pictures we have shown you over the years. In fact they are staying at that place on this trip."

John took his cue, "Please feel free to come by or to call if you need anything at all or just want to sit in familiar surroundings on the little front deck and watch the ocean."

"That is very kind," Jeanie said. "Perhaps we will take you up on that offer."

Jamison took the cue. "Johnson, can you and Mom take care of the ladies? And I will get John and Erica to their car and on their way."

"Of course." Johnson replied and the group separated to their different destinations.

****

"It is a sad thing." Jamison started as soon as they were out of ear shot. "Mr. Arthur and Mrs. Samantha were here not quite a year ago and he was dying then. But, he wanted to give her one last good memory."

"That is so sad and so sweet!" Erica said with a obvious catch in her voice as John nodded his agreement.

"Wait, there is more." Jamison stopped a moment and they all turned to face each other expectantly. "His last wish was to have an Irish style wake down here on Eleuthra and that is why she is back and why Jeanie is with her."

Erica reached over and placed her hand on John's arm. "John, you have to help them do this. You know, organize it with them . . ." then shifting her focus to Jamison, ". . . Little Johnny is really a most excellent organizer and he knows how to set things up with backup plans so that everything always, always goes the way it is supposed to go."

"I did not know this about you, John." Jamison said. "Is this something you would consider? I am sure the ladies are under stress and would appreciate the assistance. I can even make the introductions to the priest at St Paul's Catholic Church for the religious portion of the service."

"Whoa, you two. We have not been asked and I do not want to intrude on a private time of mourning. Let's take this one step at a time, shall we?" John told them in a firm voice that seemed to slow things down a bit.

"Yes, of course, you are right." Erica said as they got to the car. John started putting the things in the back of the vehicle and Erica turned to Jamison and mouthed silently, "You check with the ladies and I will work on John." Jamison gave her a thumbs-up.

****

Across town as Johnson and Mom got Samantha settled, it became clear there was some frustration that contributed to a general feeling of helplessness. Gladys, otherwise known as "Mom," went up to the room with Jeanie and Samantha. Johnson retrieved her bag .

By the time he got Samantha's few travel items upstairs with the help of a bellboy he did not need or want, the ladies were sitting together in a small tight group around the edge of the sofa. He tipped the bellboy and thanked him.

Closing the door to the hotel room quietly he faced the three women. Mom looked to him for help and he could see on her face that she was distressed. It quickly became clear why she was distressed as Jeannie and Samantha seemed to be taking turns alternately gaining control over their emotions and losing control to their emotions.

Mom pulled him into the middle of things with her words, "Johnson, these ladies need some help. You can see that they are distressed at the loss of a husband and a friend and the loss of a father." Then before he, or anyone else for that matter, could speak she added, "They need help organizing this wake that was Mr. Art's last request."

Mom continued, "You can see they are dealing with grief and are in no shape to do what has to be done to make the wake he wanted into a reality. You're my man and you've got to do something to help them."

****

There it was, he thought. She has just made this into my problem. But what he said was, "Of course, Mom, we will do everything we can to make this event a smooth and worthy celebration of the life of a fine man."

Then, shifting the conversation just a little he said, "Mom, why don't we get out of here and let these ladies rest?" as he reached out his hand to help her up from the chair she was perched on across from the sofa. Mom took his hand and allowed him to lead her to the door.

****

They were about two thirds of the way to the door when Jeanie stopped them with her words, "Mom, did you hear that young couple, Erica and John offer help? You know at the airport as Samantha was arriving."

Johnson answered before Mom could, "Yes, that's 'Little Johnny' and we have come to know him pretty well over the years. Why do you ask?"

"Well Jeannie said, Erica offered for him to help us out. I was just wondering if you really knew him?"

This time Mom spoke up first and took control of the conversation. "Girl, let me tell you. John is a real gentlemen and not afraid to take on a problem. When he was here with the divers from that school they were attending, there was one boy who was a real bully. He was a big macho man with all the muscles and he was making fun of John as being 'little' and not a real man."

Johnson added, "He was the one who started calling our friend 'Little Johnny' as a way of teasing and insulting him. Well, Johnny just took it and never got angry until the bully got rough with one of the girls one night at a local bar."

Mom spoke up again, "Well as this bully was yelling at the girl, Johnny got in between them and the big fellow pushed the girl down . . ."

John interrupted, "Pushed, no Mom, the bully hit her and knocked her down, I heard. Anyway, Johnny mopped the floor with this bully. It seems he knows some sort of jujitsu or judo or something."

"Well, the important part of the story," Mom took control of the conversation again, "came when the girl walks over to this big braggart and said to him, 'Little Johnny' huh, right now he looks kike the only real man around here and she poured her drink on the bully and walked out. But here's the point, yes we know Little Johnny and he is a quiet man who is not afraid of a challenge and who will do whatever he thinks is right in a difficult situation." And with that she stopped and folded her arms across her ample bosom.

Johnson got the last word, "Little Johnny is some kind of banker or something in Virginia and he has a reputation for always having a 'plan B' in everything he does. Does that help you?" he asked Jeannie.

Jeanie looked back at Sam who was also listening now and a look passed between them. Jeanie spoke again, but her remarks were aimed at Sam, "Maybe we should take them up on the offer Erica made at the airport and ask John to help us."

****

At the cottage the next day, Erica and John were enjoying a leisurely morning on the little deck on the front of the cottage when they heard a man's voice from around the building.

"Little Johnny! Erica! It's Johnson with some ladies, can we come and talk to you?"

John and Erica looked at each other a little confused but John stood and walked to the edge of the porch and looked along the side of the house where the big man's voice had come from. "Johnson, to what do I owe the honor of this visit this morning?" John asked.

"Little Johnny," Johnson began, "There may be some free beer in this for you so please listen and hear me out."

John continued along the side of the house between the shady palm trees and greeted Johnson with a handshake as he ushered his friend and the three ladies to the sunning deck that was more spacious than the porch on the front of the place.

Erica came over from the porch and joined them arranging the chairs for everyone to sit. Then Mom went with Erica to make a pot of coffee for the group. This left Samantha, Jeanie and Johnson outside with John.

"John," Johnson started, "I have never been to this house before. It is truly beautiful. I can see why you and Erica keep coming here. This is where you met Mr. Art and Samantha?"

Sam answered before John could, but she aimed her comments to Jeanie, "Your dad and I spent many happy hours here alone but never lonely, if you know what I mean."

"Sam, I can see why you kept coming here. It is every bit as beautiful as the pictures." Jeanie responded.

John could sense why they were here and Johnson had as much as said it when he mentioned free beer along with his initial greeting. That told John that Johnson being pressured from Mom and that they were here to get something from him or get him to do something.

He also knew that Mom was in the house right now with Erica soliciting her help in whatever they wanted. But nobody would say anything abut the real purpose of the visit until the coffee was served. So they made small talk as John reflected on how a negotiation is always a negotiation and all follow the same rules and patterns. This was not that different from his work every day at the bank.

****

Mom and Erica came back out in a few minutes with the fresh coffee and cups and both ladies were smiling. Well, John thought to himself, if Mom and Erica have agreed I guess I am doing whatever they want.

They served the coffee and talked another few minutes about the view and the quiet and the wonderful day even though it was under a sad circumstance for Samantha and Jeanie.

About half way through the cup of coffee Jeanie shifted forward in her chair, "John, we coerced Johnson to bring us here in order to ask you to do something."

John thought to himself "finally" but what he said out loud was, "I was serious with the offer at the airport to help. I feel as though I owe Samantha because when she and Art let me see this place, that is what inspired me to bring Erica here. This is where we got serious and where she agreed to marry me. I credit the surroundings and the beautiful view for her saying yes."

Erica touched his arm and all the ladies smiled at that comment. But Johnson spoke, "Little Johnny, you sound like a romantic and you are making me look bad here in front of these ladies." That brought a polite laugh but it also erased any remaining tension among the group.

Jeanie was speaking again, "Sam and I are trying to fulfill the last wishes of a man we both loved and who we miss terribly. Frankly we are overcome and spent most of the night crying together."

"So what is it you need me to do?" John asked softly.

Sam answered, "Art wanted an Irish wake or something close to that and we are asking you to interrupt your vacation and take it on for us."

John raised a hand to stop her but she pressed on as if she were afraid he would say no.

"Normally we could figure it out. I mean, I run a business in the States and Jeanie is a very accomplished, woman as well but . . ."

John stopped her this time with one soft word, "Yes."

"Did you say yes?" Jeanie interrupted.

"Yes, I would be honored to do this for you two and for Arthur." Then less seriously and with a little smile, "And for the free beer that Johnson offered when he walked up here.

That got another polite laugh as Mom and Erica poured everyone another cup of coffee. They discussed the ceremony and what Art would have liked and in the end Little Johnny and Erica said goodbye to the group.

****

When it was just the two of them and the cottage and the ocean Erica said, "I am so proud of you and I love you so much."

****

Three days later at the little church looking out on

212

the bay the Priest presided over a Mass in memory of Arthur. And everyone moved outside for the celebration of his life. The adopted group of friends listened intently as Samantha finished her remarks.

"Art brought me out into the real world of affection and taking risks with the support of ones you love and the world of with sharing with them. "You see, without him I would not exist as I am now, so he is never really gone. He is here with me now making me who and what I am. Do I miss him? Yes of course. I miss his touch and his laugh and his warmth and his supportive and wise nature."

There was not a completely dry eye in the group as she continued, "I think it was all that time in the Army. He saw a lot of death and bad things before I met him and those gave him a deep and wise perspective, like a very old person has. But he lived everyday to its fullest and he gave me one last gift I will always cherish."

She paused just a moment, "Last year he gave me that last visit here to this place with him as a 'whole man' knowing it would wear him down faster, but knowing he could give me one more lasting memory. After that he went quickly and he never complained."

"In fact his last words were an apology. He said to me, 'I am so sorry I will not make your next birthday party. Please forgive me.' Those were his last words."

Wiping her own eyes she said, "So, the least I could do was to fulfill his last wish for a wake here on the island. Even if his ashes are in Williamsburg. Today is my birthday and, you see, he was wrong. He did make it after all! He is here in my heart and in the hearts and memories of all of you who touched our lives in all those visits to this lovely island and the many precious days and nights we spent in that little cottage on the beach. Those are in my heart forever. So, everyone, please raise a glass with me and toast Art in this celebration of his life."

****

Thanks for sharing your time with me, I sincerely hope you enjoyed the story.

~*Mitch Bouchette*

mitchbouchette@gmail.com

Mitch Bouchette is quite a remarkable and versatile writer who publishes in multiple genres. He has a keen wit and a lifetime of travel experience that lends an air of authenticity to his work. Besides, he may be the first Redneck, Hispanic-Cajun, Irishman you have ever run across who was born in South Carolina. His stories will grab your head and your heart as the characters come alive on the page.

If you enjoy romance novels, please take a look:

THE SMELL OF RAIN: A Romance As It Should Be: Mitch brings you into a world of the beauty of love off the beaten path, on the island of Eleuthra, Bahamas – in his favorite getaway – The Pink Sand Cottage. This place is magical and the stories will touch your heart as the vignettes unfold, tempestuous and sometimes sad, and he will touch your heart as only he can. Have a glass of wine and enjoy!

FEEL THE RAIN: A Romance Rekindled As It Should Be: Mitch Bouchette takes us to Topsail Island, NC where Sara Brown, a successful lawyer from Virginia who is coming off of a messy divorce. She returns to Topsail where she grew up as a girl to find herself and recover control of her life. What she finds is her High School sweetheart, himself a widower, who has deep feelings for her. The appearance of her Ex-husband complicates things as the roller coaster that is her life picks up speed.

AFTER THE RAIN: Love In The Time Of COVID: Mitch introduces us to Thad and Molly who are both headed to the same house on the Outer Banks. Molly and her kids are headed to the OBX to join her BFF from college for a three-week holiday. Thad, her BFF's divorced older brother is headed there early to prep for a family gathering and he is not on board with Molly and her kids joining the family vacation. Then the bridges are closed due to COVID and they are thrown together for three weeks and things get interesting.

On the other hand if you enjoy a bit more action, please check out these titles.

THE SWORD OF RULE: Newen and Izel: What if I told you a story of Vikings raiding in Central America? Mitch Bouchette tells a tale of conquest, treason and love as only he can! The action adventure and romance pulls the reader into the lives of three couples separated by thousands of miles and thousands of years. The story will capture your imagination as the modern day Museum Director connects with her boyfriend's discoveries on a glacier 2000 years later with the conflict between Newen from Yokot'an and the Viking Aenar.

GAELIN'S RAID: Sword Of Rule Viking Series (Book 2): Mitch pulls the reader into a world of adventure, conquest and action. This is the story of Irish Vikings and explorers whose lives intertwine across the centuries. The result is a linkage of civilizations of different peoples and different cultures that developed on different continents. It ties them together across different ages from 850 AD to modern times in a heart warming and sometimes explosive story.

And if you might enjoy an irreverent and unlikely peek into "coming of age" of young men educated at The Citadel these might suit your taste.

SOUTHERN RULES (Book 1): If you grew up in the 60s, Vietnam was more than a name on a map and Civil Rights was more than just a history lesson. Southern Rules is the story of young men attending The Citadel and learning to deal with the realities of that era – from first loves to race confrontations to preparing for service in Vietnam and the Hippie counter-culture. The story will make you laugh and perhaps cry on occasion but you will identify with the characters and the crazy world they experienced.

MORE SOUTHERN RULES (BOOK 2): is a work of fiction involving the same improbable characters of the 1960s and 1970s coming together in Vietnam and Germany. The story of these young military officers comes to life against historically accurate events. If you are a child of the 60s and 70s then the Vietnam War, the Civil Rights Movement, terrorism in Germany and the craziness that made up your world is more than just a place on a map or a history lesson. This book is written for YOU so sit back and enjoy the story to relive your memories of the era.

And the new action/spy adventure series - Tango #5.

TANGO SECTION OPERATIVE #5 (BOOK 1) RESCUE FROM IRAN: In 1979 the world is in a special kind of turmoil with tensions in the Middle East, Germany is divided East and West, and the Soviet Union USSR is alive and well. Tango Section is an obscure group of operatives who are sent to work specific high interest cases . . . any way the can! Meet Charles Travis Lemon; Tango Section Operative Five – Tango 5.

TANGO SECTION: SURVIVAL! (BOOK 2): It is 1985 and the world continues to be a very dangerous place; someone is killing Tango Section Operatives. Putin is in Dresden, East Germany, and Gorbachev is not yet in charge in Russia. Tango #5 survives a car bomb in Istanbul while someone wounds his lover in Spain. Charles Travis Lemon is fed up and on task to "fix the problem" any way he can!

Made in the USA
Middletown, DE
01 March 2023